And Ghosts Are Real Too

Previous anthologies by Northants Writers' Ink

Tales of the Scorpion, 2015

While Glancing out of a Window, 2016

Talking without being Interrupted, 2017

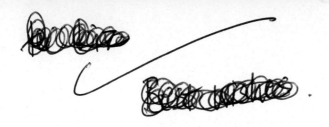

And Ghosts
Are Real Too

an anthology

by Northants Writers' Ink

edited and introduced by

Michael J Richards

Chair, Northants Writers' Ink

Monsters are real, and ghosts are real too.

They live inside us, and sometimes, they win.

– Stephen King

Contents

Introduction

Michael J Richards

This truly fine set of short stories is the fourth anthology from Northants Writers' Ink, a writers' group based in Wellingborough, Northamptonshire, England. Set in the county or slightly beyond, they tackle ghost, horror, paranormal or crime themes.

And Ghosts Are Real Too is in two parts.

Part 1 features historical stories, ranging from the tenth to the nineteenth centuries, arranged in chronological order according to their period setting.

Stories in Part 2 are set in the present day.

Part 1: historical stories

We open with "Mord um Fivewells" by **Allan Shipham**, a haunting exploration of what drives the human psyche at conscious and subconscious levels to survive, despite whatever it may face. Although it is set in tenth century Wendelingburgh, the story has resonances for contemporary readers. "Mord um Fivewells" is Allan's best story to date.

"Will", by **Michael J Richards**, the editor of this anthology, is set in 1450 or thereabouts at the time of the building of the Tithe Barn in Wellingborough – or

3

"Wendlingburgh", as the town, by then, was then called. The story follows the life of Will, a stonemason's apprentice, as the barn is constructed, and shows how he is commanded by the Will of God.

Rosalie J Weller's "Mila Goes to Granny's House" is an enchanting ghost story for children set in the village of Isham. It is set in two periods: present-day England and that of the Gunpowder Plot. This is Rosalie's first published story with Northants Writers' Ink, making her a welcome, talented new voice. "Mila Goes to Granny's House" is a thoroughly charming piece.

In "Will Ye Choose to Live?", by **Pat Aitcheson**, Ben finds himself transported back to the Battle of Naseby of 1645, a decisive battle in the English Civil War. Set in Earls Barton, Ecton and Naseby – of course – the story shows ghosts as inspirations for transformation and hope, making "Will Ye Choose to Live?" an unusual ghost story – and all the more enjoyable for that.

But then we turn to "The Betrayal", by **James Dart**. Also set in Northampton in 1645, the story shows the darker side of the period. Matthew Hopkins, self-appointed Witchfinder General, visits the town to search out and persecute women accused of sorcery. "The Betrayal" takes a sideview, though: how did the husbands of those women come to terms with their witchcraft? This carefully constructed story had me genuinely frightened.

And, for the final story in Part 1 of this anthology, we move to Kirby Hall in Corby and "Shelter from the Storm", by **Chris Wright**. Martha, her father and brother take in a bedraggled and wretched stranger from a howling storm, give him shelter and nurse him to health. But then things, inevitably, go wrong. "Shelter from the Storm" is a well characterised, violent yet nuanced story.

Part 2: contemporary stories

Deborah Bromley opens Part 2 of *And Ghosts Are Real Too* with "The Biddenham Ghosts". Set in the village of Biddenham, just over the Northamptonshire border, it tells of a young girl haunted and visited by ghosts. Written with sympathy and understanding, "The Biddenham Ghosts" shows ghosts as helpful and compassionate beings, not nasty, spiteful creatures. It's a heart-warming piece, beautifully put together.

Then we come to three stories by **N M Wogden**: "The Wellingborough Witch and the King of Croyland", "… and the Mysterious Monks", "… and the Crone in the Chair." They're cruel, they're unexplained and, in parts, very funny. This is the second new and talented voice in this anthology and is warmly welcomed.

Gordon Adams's "The Ghost Writer" begins easily enough. A writer visits a client who wants his life story written. And that starts professionally enough. As these things do. But then it goes a bit wrong. As these things do… it's a ghost story, after all.

Jason McClean takes us into crime with "Winners and Losers". Terry wins a million pounds on the lottery. So far, so good. But then everyone wants a share. Of course they do. This story looks at one man's way to dealing with the demands of his very greedy family.

We close with "The Afterparty", a short piece by James Dart. A drunken end to a sobering set of stories.

*****

Formed in October 2013, Northants Writers' Ink is a writers' group based in Wellingborough, Northamptonshire, England.

Previous anthologies are *Tales of the Scorpion* (2015), *While Glancing out of a Window* (2016) and *Talking without being Interrupted* (2017), available from good online booksellers in book and Kindle versions. More details can be found at the end of this book.

Interested new members can find more information about the group and how to join at www.northantswritersink.net, by emailing northantswritersink@outlook.com or by going to www.meetup.com.

Michael J Richards
Wellingborough, Northamptonshire
August 2018

Part 1: Historical Stories

Mord um Fivewells

Allan Shipham

The light dropped as the autumn sun moved behind storm clouds just above the horizon in the Nyn valley. The traders needed to make camp for the night. The longboat creaked as Leif, the look-out, shifted across the deck to look for a landing place on the riverbank. The valley was fertile and would provide a good resting place for the night. Beyond the bank, the plain stretched some distance where it met heavy forest and climbed the hills that surrounded them.

Loki broke his rhythm, nudged Harald and pointed at two wild boars hypnotically looking toward them from the forest edge.

"We camp on the north bank tonight!" said Leif. "There are trees we can tether to, and the currents are slow in the shallows."

Bryan, the skipper, threw back his bear skin cape, took a deep breath and scanned the tree line.

"This is known to some as Fivewells. We've camped here before. There's a small settlement to the north. See the scorch patterns in the meadow? People have made camp here recently." He turned to Loki. "Loki, we have fresh fish and several fowl, but perhaps you can find us a beast to roast before the storm gets here. The holumenn will make shelter."

"Boar or deer?" Loki mused. "It'll be good to stretch

our legs!"

A spectrum of autumn leaves stretched away into the hills, and as they drew close to the bank, the shrubbery revealed its harvest of berries. The starboard oarsmen looked up the slow-moving river and could see where Leif intended to moor the longboat. They slowed their rhythm, raised their oars and allowed those at port to manoeuvre the boat closer to the bank. As they drifted into the edge, they could feel the boat lift as the bottom rode over a submerged object. As there was no jolt or jar, they knew it was only the riverbed or a harmless silt bank under the water.

The crew stowed their oars and a couple readied the landing planks. Leif jumped on to the bank with a rope to help guide the bow in. As the boat came to rest, he tied the rope around a tree and secured it once the stern had also landed safely. The men disembarked and started to set up camp.

They were losing light, but the beasts were not that far away. Loki grabbed his bow and deer skin quiver, Harald picked up his favourite axe, and they were on the hunt. The pair followed a cart track that led towards the Fivewells settlement. Some way up, they then turned right on to a footpath into the forest. Their plan was to head off the boars and chase them on to the plain.

As they went deeper into the woods, they listened out for boar noises or any other feast-worthy animal. Through the trees ahead, they could see the forest rise off the plain and they climbed to higher ground. As they descended the other side, they could hear and then found a small stream.

They noticed fresh hoof prints in the mud where animals had recently crossed. They heard a faint squeal. Both froze and stared hard into the woodland looking for movements or other tell-tale signs.

Again, a squeal, but this time it was closer! With luck, they might be able to trap the boars without much of a hunt. They were the best and most experienced hunters among the long boat crew but sometimes it was all about luck.

Loki tested the breeze direction with a wet finger. He signalled to Harald to advance around the trees to his left and approach the boars from behind. Harald could then spook the animals, they'd run in the direction of Loki, who could then pick them off as they bolted past. This strategy had worked before and gained the men a good reputation.

Harald dropped his club, made his way, careful not to tread on twigs. He kept low to the ground, but paused briefly when he disturbed a wood pigeon that had settled down to roost. Luckily, the boars didn't seem to be alarmed.

Harald reached his optimum position. He'd lost sight of Loki, but knew he'd be waiting with bow and arrow at the ready. He heard snorts ahead of him and knew time was short, so he stood up and moved forwards, thrashing the brushes and hacking at saplings with his axe.

Loki heard Harald and pulled tighter on his bow.

The boars had dismissed the wood pigeon, but they jumped to their feet as soon as they heard the disturbance. It was a natural reflex. There were many predators in the forest and in the past they'd escaped attacks from wolves, bears and, of course, man. They'd learned many times how to save their bacon, and they bolted off into the forest away from Harald's kerfuffle. Harald gave chase when he heard movement. Undergrowth was tossed into the air, and there was squealing and snorting as the beasts fled for their lives.

The boars headed downstream of their position. Loki had misjudged and expected them to run towards him. The ground grumbled with the stampede of two, possibly three, animals but he couldn't fire his arrow as he knew Harald would be in pursuit. He lowered his weapon and joined the chase.

Loud squeals alerted other wildlife of the apparent danger. Roosting birds scattered and, as he charged ahead, Loki noticed red squirrels, hares and rabbits making for cover. Some of the animals would have made a tasty snack, but the boars were a bigger prize.

Loki ran with his bow with an arrow braced but pointing to the ground should he need to kill. As he ran, his right foot landed in the opening of a rabbit hole, his leg twisted and he dropped to the ground like a grain-filled sack. An arrow sprung unexpectedly from his bow and soared into the canopy.

Unaware, Harald continued to chase.

* * * * *

Harald had expected to see a downed animal with an arrow in its chest or even Loki chasing through the bushes, but there was nothing. He wondered if Loki had crafted a new plan and would be further down the gulley. A lone arrow ripped through the air in front of him and came to rest in a tree. He caught sight of the animals ahead as they briefly rested. They looked around sniffing at the air, watching for movement. As Harald slowly stalked the animals, he raised his axe so he could throw it if he got close enough. For no apparent reason, the boars were spooked again and charged off towards a rocky scree ahead. Harald briefly glanced back for his companion but continued his pursuit.

As the boars ran toward the scree, one peeled off and disappeared into the rocks. The others bolted further into the forest out of sight. Harald grew tired and slowed down to catch his breath. The smaller boars were lost, but he looked to see where the larger one had gone. As he approached the scree, he could see the rock face had been recently excavated from the hillside and appeared to be a local source of coal. There had been collapses of soil and rock and several openings where caves had been hacked into the hill.

Harald approached with extreme caution.

Unidentifiable noises came from inside one of the caves. It was too dark to see deep into the cave. Harald decided to take a few steps into the darkness to see if the boar ran out when he went in.

Loki grabbed him by the shoulder and Harald gasped.

"You startled me!"

"Why are you going in there?" asked Loki.

"One of the beasts went inside. We can chase it out."

"You know to never go into caves you're not familiar with, especially without a torch. Don't remember Fivewells having caves? How did you find these?"

"The boar led us here."

"I twisted my ankle. I can walk but it's really sore!" Loki rotated his leg carefully. "We'd best head back. The storm is closing and we're losing daylight.

"Ready your bow and I'll go in."

"Harald, let's go. We can snare hares or bag some squirrels on the way back. Magnus can make some broth."

"This boar will provide not only a feast for tonight, but breakfast for the morrow."

Harald started into the dark.

Loki raised his bow and arrow and nodded. "Be sure and let me know when you are heading back out. I don't want to shoot you."

* * * * *

Back at camp, the first rain started to fall. Droplets bounced off the canvas-covered frames. Thunder rumbled in the distance.

A young man being tattooed moved deeper under cover as the rain crept into the entrance to the tent. Some oarsmen had tied down canvases on the boat and busied themselves distributing blankets and sleeping pelts. Two men hammered a tap into a barrel of ale, while others waited with drinking horns. One of the oarsmen raised his hood against the weather and stoked the raging fire that awaited Loki's and Harald's prize.

"Hamm Tun is only hours away. We should make market in good time if we rise early. Soon the snows will be here. The river will freeze. We'll have to wait for the thaw to come back to trade."

14

There was a loud shriek as a lone hunter emerged from the forest and limped across the plain. Several men grabbed their weapons and started across the meadows, unsure of the fate before them. A couple sprinted ahead to meet the dishevelled man. Loki saw his colleagues running toward him, took a few weak paces and fell to the ground.

* * * * *

Loki woke and looked at a circle of faces bearing down on him. Troy, the barber, tended his wounds with a poultice and wrapped washed leaves around his arm.

"What happened, Loki?"

"What... Where?"

"You were hunting with Harald. You weren't gone long... " Troy pressed the poultice hard to a wound on Harald's neck. "We made camp awaiting your return, but you emerged from the woods alone and torn to pieces."

"Harald!" Loki sat upright.

"We can't find him. We have people looking, but it's dark and we don't know where to look."

A novice barber arrived with some leeches in a wooden bowl.

"Were you attacked? Where is Harald?"

"We need to save Harald!" Loki said.

Troy swigged ale from a horn and threw the rest over Loki's scratches. He smarted as the ale braced the open wounds.

"He's delirious, he may be possessed," said one of the onlookers.

Several boatmen touched talismen and started muttering with their heads bowed.

"Pass the leeches!" said Troy.

Loki fell unconscious again.

* * * * *

As Loki stirred, he could hear the men talking around a fire. He sat up sharp and noticed dressings around the wounds on his arms and neck. He tried to stand but fell back into a sitting position. His head was sore but he felt well enough to join the others. As he tried again to get to his feet, he noticed on the back of his hands tell-tale circular marks where Troy had feasted his leeches and drained away the evil spirits.

"Loki stirs!" a young member of the crew called. Some of the boatmen got up and crossed to the shelter.

"Are you well?" asked Troy from several paces.

"Better! What of Harald?"

"We gave up the search. There was no sign of him in the dark."

As he stepped out from the shelter, Loki stooped after putting weight on his weak ankle. The storm had passed. Everything was rain-soaked so the men sat around a camp fire, told stories and drank.

He limped over to the circle and was passed a horn of ale.

"Drink well, Loki. My leeches have done their work. You'll feel better in the morning. For now, fill yourself with this foul soup and good spirits. Are you well enough to remember what happened on your hunt?"

"Yes! Did Harald return?" His voice was frail but his words were clear.

A boisterous crewman who had drank several ales rose to his feet.

"I will go to him now in the woods and bring him back."

"Don't be a fool! Whoever attacked them nearly killed Loki and we don't know where Harald is. We'll resume the search in the morning, once Loki leads us to where they went."

"We were by the coal-cast excavations!"

"There're no coal mines in Fivewells!"

"It was freshly dug. Someone must have excavated since we last traded here."

"Tomorrow, we can check out your coal-cast and maybe take some back with us."

"You will have to get past the beast first."

Everyone went quiet when Loki spoke. Earnestly, he glanced around the circle at the shocked faces.

"Of what beast do you speak? Wild boar?" one teased.

"Harald and I stalked boars through the forest. One ventured toward the rocks and into the caves. We lost trail of the others, so we went after the one in the cave."

"What happened next?"

"It was dark, so Harald went to the entrance and looked inside, hoping he could see, or spook the boar out. We both heard strange... noises from inside, but dismissed them. They weren't loud or fierce enough to be wolf or bear and I imagined it was some creaking timbers or

17

shifting rocks from inside the excavations.

"I'd twisted my ankle so I stood some way back, poised with my bow and arrow to strike the beast as it emerged. Suddenly, a monster came out of the dark. It was twice the size of Magnus, and twice as tall. He was angry we'd disturbed him and raged, his paws ripping the rock from the wall."

"A bear?" offered Leif.

"This was no bear! No bear, I tell you!" He shook his head fiercely and confidently. "I have faced off bear before. This was no bear! Its eyes were piercing, fire red in the shadows of dusk. Blood fell from its razor white teeth and its nostrils flared when it growled."

"Fire red eyes?" Leif repeated, sniffing Loki's breath.

"Yes! It had the face of an angry man and the body and fur of a bear. It walked tall, like a man, but its lethal claws were the biggest I've ever seen. As it attacked Harald, it looked around at me, searching for its next victim. It was like it didn't care about Harald, he was just in its way."

"What happened to Harald?"

"After several swipes of its claws, Harald was thrown through the air backwards by the animal. It had the strength of ten oarsmen. Afterwards, it roared to show his worth. Harald hit an old oak tree with a thud, went limp and dropped to the floor. For all I know, he's still there."

"Poor Harald!"

"You left him there?"

"No! I was scared he'd be attacked again by the animal, so I fired off two arrows at the animal's torso. They struck him in his shoulder, but the animal just tore them out, broke them and cast them into the bracken. I've never seen anything like it before."

Loki dropped and sat on a stool fashioned from a sawn tree trunk.

"By the gods! I swear I did all I could. The animal growled again in a way I'd not seen. It started in my direction, I was able to get another arrow off, but it missed its chest and hit its arm. This seemed to make it even angrier. Its march toward me turned into a canter. I was petrified. The animal reached me, knocked my bow to the ground and growled in my face. It grasped an arrow from my quiver and snapped it in front of me. It just hung there staring right at me, waiting for a response. I overcame my fear and backed away slowly."

"What happened next?"

"I had to do something! Harald had left the club near where I was. I reached around to grab it and I'm sure the monster knew what I was going to do. As I swung the club around with all my strength, it reached out and stopped it in its path. I thought I was going to die.

"It pushed me backwards and I lost my grip on the club. As I fell to the ground, I could see whatever it was still held the club. It threw the club off into the woods and I never heard it hit the ground. I tried to escape the attack by crawling into the undergrowth."

"How did you get away?"

"The thing… it just kept coming. It grabbed at my legs and knocked me to the ground, then it ripped at my arms and neck. I could feel agonising pain as its claws ripped through my skin, but a few moments later I was still alive. I could feel blood from my wounds creep across my skin, warm against the cool air, and I started to feel faint. Next, I could feel myself being picked up and thrown through the air – like Harald. As I travelled through the air, time stood still and I could see all around into the darkness, every tree and every bush. I couldn't see Harald or the animal, as they were behind me. I've never been so scared in my life. I wanted to scream but could make no noise. I saw the ground approaching as I crashed into it. It was awful. All went black and I don't remember any more. Not until I woke last night with everyone around me. I have no idea how I got back to camp."

"You speak of a mythical demon beast, half-man, and half-bear?" said Bryan.

"I only tell you what I saw!"

"There was no beast, I say!" replied Bryan.

"What of Harald?" Leif said.

"No doubt, Harald met an accident in the woods and Loki has concocted this story to make him out to be a brave warrior!"

"I have not – "

"Enough! Now there's light, we'll sweep the woods and try to find out what's happened. Lead us to this coal-cast so we can confirm your story."

* * * * *

Some remained to dismantle the camp, but most headed off into the woods to find Harald. Loki led the way from memory.

"Look for Loki's bow and quiver and Harald's axe. They may be clues to Harald's location."

"It was darker, but I think it's this way!" said Loki.

The search party descended a hill to a small stream and crossed it.

"The coal-cast is ahead," Loki said. "We stalked three boars from the high ground on the left down this gorge towards the east. One strayed to the left and into the excavations."

"Be on your guard, men," the skipper said. "We may be dealing with Loki's demon. Leave no stone unturned and no clue lost. Harald may still be alive, in pain or in slumber."

The men were vigilant in their search.

"Skipper!" one of the men shouted. "I think I've found the axe! It has blood on it!"

"Bring it here!"

"It can't be Harald's axe," Loki said. "I never used it in the fight."

"It's clear someone has!" said Bryan, examining the weapon. "The polished blade has a line of dried blood along the cutting edge. If it had been used to attack a human or an animal, it would have left a scar."

"I don't understand!"

"Just because you don't remember something, Loki, doesn't mean it didn't happen," said one of the others.

"So what did happen?"

"That is what we're here to find out."

"Skipper!" another one of the search party shouted. The others crowded his find.

"My bow and quiver! They're destroyed – " Before him were the dismembered parts of his beloved possession. " – and all my arrows are gone!"

"Who would do this?" puzzled Bryan.

"It must have been the monster!" Loki replied. "I didn't lose it here, I was over there. Someone or something moved it."

They continued through the woods and came on a clearing in front of the scree, on the side of the hill. Someone had dug into the scree creating an open coal-cast excavation, as Loki had described. This had created several shallow caves. They appeared to be abandoned and didn't appear to have been very fruitful, the spoil scattered all around.

"It was in here!" Loki beckoned with his arm.

"Careful… Weapons at the ready!"

Loki and Leif were the first to enter. There wasn't much to see. It was an abandoned excavation. At their feet was the freshly disembowelled body of a wild boar, probably the one Loki and Harald had hunted.

"Here is the evidence!" Loki insisted. "Why would Harald and I do this? This beast would've been better butchered at camp. I wonder where Harald can be!"

"This is the work of an imbecile, that's all. There's no evidence of any demon beasts here."

"Harald!" Loki shouted into the woods, but there was no return.

"Spread out!"

"Skipper… in the trees overhead! Harald's club."

Everyone looked to the canopy overhead. Sure enough,

the club Loki had used was in the branches of a tree. A couple of the crew threw small branches to knock it down, but their efforts were futile and they soon gave up.

"There's no way I could have thrown it up there!"

"There is definitely a mystery here, Loki. That much is true."

They continued their search.

Further into the woods, Bryan found Harald, lying on the ground, lifeless and ripped to pieces by something very sharp. The undergrowth around him was disturbed, as if there had been a struggle. A single arrow stood proud of his face, embedded in his left eye socket. His face bore a sickened grimace.

"It looks like he was pinned to the floor when he was killed."

"Maybe he was standing up when the arrow hit him and he fell backwards?"

"Just maybe a stray arrow from an archer in the dark hit his companion, not his prey!" said Bryan.

"No! That's not what happened!" pleaded Loki.

"Seize him! I've heard enough!"

"But… but… "

"You were trusted to lead the hunt, your companion died and you didn't feed the crew. You've failed!"

"Skipper! I'm innocent!"

"You are to stand trial for the murder of Harald. When we make camp tonight, you will carry the iron and we'll see who's innocent."

Several of the crew grabbed hold of Loki and led him back to the boat kicking and protesting.

"Carry Harald back to the boat. We must prepare his journey to the afterlife. We'll go to Hamm Tun for the market and set a pyre adrift later when we reach the sea on our journey home."

Watching from the distance, a creature with what resembled a human face jerked an arrow in the air several times with its right hand. With its left hand, it carefully nursed a single axe wound to its thigh. The wound shallow and would heal with time.

Will

Michael J Richards

The Tithe Barn, Crowland Abbey, Wendlingburgh, the County of Northampton
Six o'clock, morning, Tuesday, 4 June, sometime between 1400-1450

"So, Will," Thomas says as they stroll across the field, the early morning sun slowly creeping up into the cloudless blue sky, "tomorrow you shall marry. Are you ready?"

"Joanna is the love of my life," Will says. "How can I not be ready?"

"Son, it makes me glad," Thomas says, patting him on the back. "Joanna is a lovely girl. And you are a fine young man."

"Thank you, Father." Grinning, Will brushes a fly away from his auburn hair. "She is busy with the other women, preparing the wedding table. I should keep away – "

"It is work for the women," Thomas says. "Why go near?"

Will stops and scratches himself between his legs. "I cannot wait to – "

His father turns to see what keeps him. "Steady, lad, do not damage yourself. I want you to give me grandchildren."

"Is it so bad to be keen to share a bed with her?" Will

laughs, his face reddening. "Is it so bad to want to be with her every hour God sends us?" He rubs himself, his broad thighs shaking. "I love her."

"I am pleased to see it," Thomas chuckles, watching him. "In the meantime, son, keep your hands off it. We have work to do."

The place is unattended. The Benedictine monks are at Early Morning Prayer. The other men and apprentices have yet to arrive. But Thomas and Will have plenty to get on with.

Inside the barn, they walk over to where several ladders are propped up in a row against the incomplete south-facing ironstone wall. As they are first to arrive, they must place the ladders at various points around the building, ready for when the others get there.

Will grips the middle ladder and pulls it back.

Thomas goes to one on the end. "Why do you always start in the middle? Makes no sense."

"Get the heaviest out the way first," Will says. "Then if the others fall, they will not hurt so much when they hit us."

"More to the point, you can show how strong you are."

"But I *am* strong!" He has the ladder away from the stonework with one hand and above his head. "Look!" He brushes his auburn hair out of his eyes with his other hand.

"I have seen your strength before, son. No need to show off."

"No," Will says. "Father, look here," he adds, carefully and quietly putting the ladder down on the dusty ground and stepping towards the wall.

Thomas rests his ladder back in its place and moves nearer. "What?"

"A man... a dead man."

"Help me clear the space. Get some light."

Slowly, one ladder at a time, the body is revealed.

"May the Lord bless us," Thomas mutters. He kneels down and turns the lifeless corpse over.

A man of some forty years stares up at him, his eyes open, his mouth gaping, his outstretched tongue resting on his lower lip. Mucous and snot cover the philtrum and upper lip. Parched blood is spread over his ears.

"It is Nicholas Baker," Thomas says.

"He makes bread, not buildings," Will says, kneeling down. "What is he doing here? Look." He points to the baker's hair, now the white of stone ground flour, strewn across the man's head as if in a high wind.

"Nicholas was a redhead," Thomas says.

"A beacon on a cloudy summer night," Will sniggers.

Thomas looks up at his son. "Better not let anyone else hear you say that." He holds up the dead man's hands, the colour of whey and buttermilk cheese left to mould. "As if once buried and now dug up." He stands up. "We cannot leave him like this. But he should not be moved. We must fetch the justice and the coroner."

"They are up in Lincoln," Will says, "not to return until tomorrow."

"For your marriage ceremony with Joanna. Let us wait for the others and then decide what is best."

"Father, I did not show Master Baker appropriate honour. I beg your pardon."

"It is forgotten."

In a few minutes, the other two masons – Masters Staines and Waller – and their apprentices, John and Peter – are in the roofless tithe barn.

"Nothing can be done," Master Staines growls. "We shall wait until tomorrow."

"At least we should find Brother Boniface," Master Waller says. "He will know what must be done."

"John," Master Staines waves his apprentice away.

John turns to go.

"Take Peter with you," Master Waller calls.

The two lads leave without a word.

"Your wedding table will be spoilt," Master Staines smirks. "No bread and sweetmeats. What will you do?"

"All will be well," Thomas says. "Do not worry."

"Me, worry? Ha! Why should I worry?" Master Staines sneers. "I don't know why he wants to marry her, anyway."

Will clenches his fists. "Sir, Joanna and I – "

But Thomas holds him back. "That is not the sort of talk we want here, Master Staines. On this day, a death. On the morrow, a wedding. Probably a burial the day after. We are guided by God's will."

"Amen, Master Bower."

"Thank you, Master Waller," Thomas says. "Will, fetch Masters Staines and Waller some ale, then some for you and myself while we await Brother Boniface. Bring some for John and Peter, also."

He hands Will some coins. Will finds the cups and a tray at the far end of the barn, where the craftsmen's tools are kept, and leaves.

"We should step outside," Thomas says. "Leave the poor man in peace. He never got much of it during his living days with that shrew of a wife. At least allow him tranquility now."

The three men step outside into the meadow, the green ground covered with dandelions and daisies.

"This grass," Master Staines says, "needs cutting. Too long by far."

"Speak to young Ben," Master Waller says. "He cut it only seven days ago. It grows too fast."

"That idle rascal? I would not hire him to cut his nose off to spite his face."

"He does a good job," Master Waller nods.

"He is only a lad," Thomas says.

Will appears at the bottom of the slope, walking slowly towards them, the tray firmly in both hands.

"A man," Thomas says, "knoweth not his end. But as fishes are taken with a hook and as birds are taken with a snare – "

" – so men," Master Waller continues, "are taken in their time, when it cometh suddenly to them."

"Amen, my good friends," Master Staines says. "Amen."

Will reaches them with the ale from the village, offers the tray. They each take a cup, Will takes his and sets the tray down.

"Ah," Thomas says. "Brother Boniface."

"My prayers were interrupted," he puffs. He is little older than Master Staines, the oldest stonemason. His heavy black habit ruffles in the breeze as he approaches them. His soft face breaks into a smile. "What matters

29

more than supplication to Our Lord?"

Will, John and Peter following behind, the four men go into the barn and to Nicholas Baker's cold, white body. Will gives John and Peter their ale.

"Aah," Brother Boniface sighs, makes the sign of the cross, puts his hands together in prayer. *"Sed et si ambulavero in valle mortis non timebo malum quoniam tu mecum es virga tua et baculus tuus ipsa consolabuntur me."* ["For though I should walk in the midst of the shadow of death, I will fear no evil, for thou art with me. Thy rod and thy staff, they have comforted me."]

He bows his head, his lips move for a while, then he lifts his face to the others. "We must leave him here until the justice and coroner arrive. No harm will come to him today. We must cover him. I will bring blankets. But – "

" – in the night – "

"In the night, as you say, Peter, the creatures will feed off him. Two of you must light a fire and stay with him through the hours of darkness so the departure of his soul is not interfered with. And then the law of the land will be followed. Who will guard his body and soul?"

No-one speaks.

"Surely two of you can find it in your hearts to care for your battered friend?"

Will looks at Thomas, who nods at the monk. "We will watch over him. We discovered him. It is our duty."

Master Staines lets out a huge sigh. Master Waller, looking at the ground, shakes his head.

"Who will tell his wife?" Thomas says. "A difficult woman."

30

Brother Boniface nods. "I will carry out that onerous task, find a shroud and flowers for him and arrange the burial. One of your apprentices will take me to her."

"I will come with you for the blankets," Will says.

"Allow me to take you to her, if I may?" John says, turning to Master Staines. "I know the family."

"So be it," Master Staines says.

"In the meantime," Brother Boniface says, "work on the barn must continue." He looks at Will and John. "Come with me. We will do what we have to, although I fear I shall be late for Terce. But no matter."

He, Will and John turn to go. Brother Boniface turns back. "God will look after us. Such is His will."

The three leave the barn.

"I am working at the far end," Thomas says. "Until Will comes back, I need one of you to help me build the scaffolding."

"I will work with you," says Master Staines. "I can do nothing until John's here."

"Peter and I," Master Waller says, "will help. Today, we should work together. Four of us will build scaffolding much quicker than two."

"Thoughtful words," Thomas says.

Peter and the other men go to the west of the building, where the wall is already some six feet high. Although they need only short, light scaffolding for the next stage, the other two lads must join them before they can build upwards. So, instead of building a short stretch, they start erecting scaffolding the length of the wall.

Will returns a little later with four blankets. Thomas

31

helps him to roll Master Baker's body to one side, lay out two blankets on the ground and place him back over them. The other two blankets cover him. They join the others, no-one speaking while they carry on building the scaffolding.

It is noon, the hot sun in mid-sky, when Mistress Unity, Master Baker's widow, Peter and Brother Boniface come into what will become Wendlingburgh's Tithe Barn. The men stop working, stand by, not coming forward. They know a widow's grief, they know the Lord's will, they know their lives are short.

"What are we to do?" she cries, falling on her knees before the covered blankets. "Who will provide for me?"

"Our Lord will provide," Brother Boniface mutters.

"He is truly mysterious," Will whispers.

"Aye, lad," Master Staines says. "Five children and now a living to make. May God help her."

Peter joins the men, leaving the weeping woman to her sorrow.

Brother Boniface goes over them. "Nicholas will be buried as soon as the law has taken its course. Probably Friday."

"That is all any of us can do," Thomas says.

"Except pray for his soul," Brother Boniface adds.

"Why should we?" Master Staines says. "He was a good man. His widow has had long enough to grieve. Let us go to her."

As they walk back, Mistress Unity is uncovering the dead man's face, leaning over and kissing her husband on the lips. She runs her hands over his features, puts the cover back and stands up.

She turns to the men. "I have children to tend to. Thank you for your kindness."

"Let me walk back with you," Brother Boniface says, coming over to her. "Will and Master Bower will look after Nicholas." He turns to Will. "I have told Joanna to bring food, blankets and fire-striking tools for your vigil tonight."

Unity smiles at them, Brother Boniface takes her arm and they leave.

For the rest of the day, the men and apprentices work, hardly speaking. Mid-afternoon, Joanna, Cranley and Gerard, her young brothers, bring food, two jugs of ale, blankets and the fire-striking tools.

"For your sacred vigil," she tells her husband-to-be.

"Can we see Master Baker's body?" Cranley asks.

"No!" Gerard laughs. "The worms will have already eaten him up."

An hour before nightfall, the men pack their tools away and, except for Thomas and Will, leave. Thomas sets about lighting a fire with the flint and blade Joanna has brought. Will lays out the blankets a few feet away from Master Baker's body, prepares some food and pours some ale. They settle down, eat and drink.

"The barn is coming on well," Will says.

It is oblong, some eighty by twenty-two feet. The lime and ironstone walls are, so far, about half the finished height.

"Yes, son, it is," his father says. "The abbot will be pleased with our work and I will be paid well."

Will stands up, walks a few yards for a satisfyingly long

piss. "How," he calls, "do you think Master Baker died?"

"I do not know, Will. His body is clean and tidy. Perhaps the Lord was ready to receive him. Anyway, the justice and coroner will carry out their work and that is nothing to do with us. Our task is to keep vigil. That is all we should concern ourselves with."

Will returns, hitching up his stockings. "When the Lord is ready to receive me, I shall go bravely. I will not shame Joanna. She will be proud of me. I have seen Death today – "

"You have seen Death before," Thomas says. "Do you not fear it?"

"You have seen Death, too. Are you not afraid?"

"Of course I am," Thomas agrees, putting down his wooden cup. "That would be the end of my life with your mother and your brothers. How can I not be afraid?"

"Because," Will says, "you will have been with us and then you will be with Our Lord. Surely that is good?"

"You are to marry Joanna tomorrow. Do you not want to spend as much time with her as possible?"

"Of course, Father. But I am strong, I have good health, I am full of seed." He rubs his groin. "My life has promise and vigour. You will have many grandchildren."

Thomas stokes the fire with a stick. "You did well today, Will. Joanna is a fortunate woman."

"It is I who has good fortune."

Dark shadows are changing into black night. The waning moon hovers. Above, an owl screeches. Somewhere, a fox barks. A rabbit scampers by, its shape captured in the fire-glow.

"Only seven hours to dawn," Thomas yawns. "Sleep for a few hours. I will shake you when I can keep awake no longer."

Will pulls a blanket over him, curls up, closes his eyes. "Joanna," he mutters.

Six o'clock, morning, Wednesday, 5 June, sometime between 1400-1450

"He is possessed by the devil."

"Will, where is Thomas? What have you done with the body of poor Nicholas? Where is it?"

"John, Peter, fetch Brother Boniface. He will know what to do."

Will lies on the ground, shaking, his knees curled up under his chin, his mouth sucking his thumb, tears streaming down his cheeks. His face is drained of colour, his hands are drenched in blood. His hair is white, the white of Joanna's wedding shift, the white of flowers at a burial, the white of candles lit for Mass, the white of winter snow, the white of the abandoned soul.

Masters Staines and Waller wrap him up with one of the now blood-covered blankets.

But, rolling over on to his stomach, Will hurls it aside. "Do not touch me! Get him off me!" He chews on the dust, bites at the dewy grass, groaning and cackling, writhing, his feet kicking out, arms and hands thumping the ground.

"What is going on, Jack?" Master Waller whines.

"Only the Lord knows, Edgar," Master Staines, whispers.

"Why is Brother Boniface taking so long?"

"He is at Early Morning Prayer," Jack says. "Again. We can do nothing until he gets here."

They step back.

"And look at that," Edgar sighs, pointing to the scaffolding. "All our work gone to nothing."

It is destroyed. Its broken pieces are strewn in shreds. Tangled, gnawed rope is scattered. The wall itself is a rubble, as if an enemy army has thrust a battering ram against it, reducing it to a heap of diabolical dust. Stones, pebbles, bricks lie everywhere, as if tossed about in a sudden mania of furious apoplexy.

"God help us."

Brother Boniface runs into the barn, Peter and John close behind. Seeing the now exhausted Will, he kneels down, turns the young man over and places his palm on Will's forehead. "Speak to me, my son. Who did this to you?"

Will opens his eyes. He opens his mouth and spits out blood. Like an angry familiar being throttled to death, his high-pitched voice screeches, *"Quis es?"* ["Who are you?"]

Brother Boniface stares at him. "I did not know Will had Latin," he calls to the stonemasons.

"He does not," Jack says. "Thomas is – "

"Where is Thomas?"

" – teaching him to read and write."

"But here he is," Brother Boniface says, "speaking perfect Latin."

"How can that be?"

"Where is Thomas? And Nicholas? What have you done with them?"

Brother Boniface grips Will by the shoulders, holding him so he is sitting up. "*Loqueris ad me, filius meus. Quis hoc fecit tibi?*" ["Speak to me, my son. Who did this to you?"]

Will laughs. Foaming, bloody saliva slavers down his chin. His widened eyes stare into the monk's soul as he chants, "*Et similitudines locustarum, similes equis paratis in prælium: et super capita earum tamquam coronæ similes auro: et facies earum tamquam facies hominum. Et habebant capillos sicut capillos mulierum: et dentes earum, sicut dentes leonum errant.*"

As Brother Boniface covers his face with his hands, Will crashes to the ground. "Oh Heaven save us!" the Benedictine monk whispers, pulling away. He stands up, his mouth wide open, his hands shaking.

"What did he say?" Edgar says. "What did he say?"

Brother Boniface shakes his head, shakes it again. He stands up straight and recites, "'And the likenesses of the locusts resembled horses prepared for battle. And upon their heads were something like crowns similar to gold. And their faces were like the faces of men. And they had hair like the hair of women. And their teeth were like the teeth of lions.'"

He stops, looks at the two masons and two apprentices. "It is from the Book of Revelation. The sound of the fifth trumpet which heralds the apocalypse." He crosses himself.

"What does it mean?" Edgar says. "What does it mean?"

"Woe, woe, woe, to those who dwell on the earth," Brother Boniface chants. "It is the first foreshadowing of

Armageddon."

Statues frozen by fear, the monk, the two stonemasons and their apprentices stand silently over Will, staring at his tortured body, studying his troubled soul. None moves, not even to brush away the gnats swarming about their heads. The sun, in its endless heat, gives them no relief. Its sharp light does not shield or protect them.

"Where is Thomas?"

No-one knows. No-one answers. No-one has an answer to give.

"Thomas!"

The name, spat out of Will's mouth, fills the unfinished building, rises up into the air, disappears in a cloudy whisper and floats away towards the deep blue sky.

He sits up, his hands outstretched, his right finger pointing at an unknown, unseen vision. His lips quiver, his shoulders shake, his legs and feet tremble so that the ground beneath him shudders.

"Our Father – "

His whole body breaks out into a waterfall of sweat and saliva. His stockings are soon soaked in urine and, before long, he lets out faecal odours. He tries to stand but falls back, his head crashing with a loud bang against the wall.

His sparkling blue eyes dilate, his white foaming mouth opens wide, his bright red tongue hangs out, his rough blackened hands reach up.

"Thy will be done – "

His back arches, his chest heaves. He takes a huge breath, lets out a rapturous, anguished sigh and falls, dead.

Mila Goes to Granny's House
a ghost story for children

Rosalie J Weller

"This is the BBC. After more than four hundred years, Robert Catesby has been exonerated from his part in the Gunpowder Plot after startling new evidence has come to light from the Palace Archives. A secret investigation was launched after a letter had been discovered from one of the conspirators to His Majesty King James I. This letter implied that the whole Gunpowder Plot debacle was a ruse to turn the country against Roman Catholic noblemen and secure England as a Protestant nation."

"That's Mary's Robert," Mila said suddenly to her daddy.

"Don't be silly, Mila. That's not someone you know. That man died over four hundred years ago."

Mila didn't argue with Daddy. That would be rude. But she did smile to herself.

One week earlier

It was Mila's turn to give her news to the class. She didn't like speaking when all eyes were on her but she knew she had to. She took the teddy bear from Lucy, declaring herself the speaker.

"After school, I have to drive with my daddy for a long time – an hour, I think. I am going to Granny's house and I will stay on my own there for the whole week."

The ordeal was nearly over. Mila sighed, pushing her long hair behind her ear just as Mummy had told her. "When you speak, make sure your hair is not in your eyes." Only the questions from the other children remained. Mila was relieved there was only one question and she could answer it with ease.

"Granny lives in Isham," she answered, "which is in Northamptonshire, uh, I think."

It was finished. Everyone clapped. She passed the teddy to Peter who liked talking and she knew his long news would give her time to recover. Masha, her friend, squeezed her hand and moved nearer to her on the carpet.

"I will miss you," Masha whispered.

The two girls enjoyed each other's company as News Time continued. Miss Bell always moved them apart because she said they talked too much when they were together. But this time Miss Bell hadn't noticed.

It was home time very soon. Mummy met Mila from school and, as she got in the car, she noticed her purple travel bag bulging next to her car seat.

"Mummy, did you remember to pack my Annabelle colouring book?"

"No, Mila," Mrs Marsh replied, "You know babushka has colouring books for you. But I remembered your new Annabelle buggy!"

Mila squealed with delight. She could walk around the square in Granny's street, pushing Annabelle in her new buggy. She loved Annabelle. Father Christmas had brought her for Mila. Masha also had an Annabelle. The girls loved their babies. Walking with their dolls made them feel grown up. It was a wonderful game.

Olga Marsh negotiated the traffic smoothly and was delighted to find her husband had managed to get home early. Mila started singing,

"Dad – dy's – home. Dad – dy's home, ee i aye addio, my daddy's home."

After several repetitions, Olga's endurance collapsed. She pulled in the driveway, unclipped Mila's seatbelt deftly and slumped in her seat. She enjoyed a moment of peace as Mila clambered out of the open door and into her daddy's arms.

The usual ritual was followed. She screamed as Daddy chased her around the house, until Mummy shouted, "That's enough!"

Soon Mila and Daddy were driving along the motorway to Granny's house.

"I like this granny so much more than Russian Granny, daddy," Mila said.

Daddy smiled.

"Well, you'd better not say that when Russian Granny is around."

"No, Daddy, I know. Some things we just say to ourselves. Are we there yet?"

"Not long now, Princess. You practise reading your book. You know how much Granny loves to hear you read."

Yes, Mila did know that. It was easy talking to Granny.

She sounded the same as Daddy and Miss Bell at school. When Mummy said the same words, they didn't sound the same. Granny reminded Mila of Daddy. She loved her daddy. Mila looked out of the window. She recognised the McDonalds as they came off the motorway.

"Daddy," Mila cried out, "we're nearly there!"

Daddy glanced backward to her. She was the brightness in his exhausting life. "Yes, we are."

The familiar terraced houses lined both sides of the road as they drove into one of the few estates in the small village of Isham, Northamptonshire. As they neared the first turning, Mila spied Granny's bungalow on the corner. Yes, there was Granny's caravan and her car.

Mila saw a girl about her age walking quickly past. She had long brown hair arranged in ringlets. She looked as if she were going to a party. The dress she wore was long to the ground and frilled in layers. Mila thought she looked so pretty.

"I wish I could have a party dress like that, Daddy," she said.

"Like what Mila? What are you talking about now, Princess?" Daddy said.

There was no time for Mila to give Daddy an explanation. As soon as the car stopped, Granny had opened the door. How did Granny know when they were there?

"Is Katie coming to your house today, Granny?"

Mila was impatient to see her older cousin and find a playmate. She wondered if the girl she had seen wanted to play.

"Not today, Princess," Daddy said before Granny could answer.

Mila was annoyed. Granny would have invited Katie to come and see her if Daddy hadn't said no so quickly.

"You know Daddy has to leave soon because he has to go to work tomorrow, don't you Mila?" Granny said.

Mila knew that. Why was Granny telling her something she already knew? When they had talked about it, both Mummy and Daddy had told her she was staying at Granny's on her own. She followed Granny and Daddy up the stairs to her room. The stairs were not the same as her stairs at home. They were narrower and deeper. She climbed carefully. She didn't want to stumble. Then they would think she was just a baby.

As they opened the bedroom door, Daddy and Granny were talking. But she wasn't listening. Her eyes were fixed on her bed. There, by the pillow, was the most beautiful doll she had ever seen. She was like Annabelle but her skin was brown and her hair was black. Was that doll for her? Who else? Katie was too old for dolls. Maybe cousin Alfred – but boys didn't usually play with dolls. She thought hard. No, she had never seen Alfred with a doll.

Daddy picked the doll up from the bed and put her in Mila's hands. "You're spoilt, Mila. Say thank you to Granny for the lovely present."

So it *was* hers. A huge smile spread across her face. "Oh, thank you, Granny."

Granny's house was smaller than Mila's but Granny's garden was bigger. It had lots of special places – little spaces you could crawl in and hide. Granny's garden

43

smelled of lavender and other garden flowers she didn't know the names of.

It was soon time for Daddy to leave. She didn't feel sad. Mila knew Daddy had to go to work the next day.

"Granny, can I go outside to play tomorrow? I am seven now."

Reassured that Granny wasn't going to treat her like a baby, Mila soon fell asleep. Her new doll slept next to her.

The next morning, Mila woke up early but waited until she heard Granny in the kitchen before getting up. She endured the fussing as Granny made sure she put on her play clothes and repeated Granny's Golden Rules: Don't leave the square; Don't talk to Grown-ups you don't know; Remember to be polite if you talk to Sienna's mother; Always say please and thank you.

Mila made her way to the bench under the tree just a few hundred yards from Granny's front door. The girl wearing the fancy dress was sitting on the bench.

"Hello," Mila said.

"Can you see me?"

"Of course, you're sitting next to me. Why wouldn't I see you?"

The girl left the question unanswered. Mila liked talking to her new friend although she didn't understand all the things she said. She kept talking about Master Robert and seemed to assume Mila knew what she was talking about. Master Robert was in trouble because of a 'spiracy. Mila didn't know what that was.

Mila was trying to be a good friend and be polite. That meant listening without interrupting.

"I'm Mary," the girl said, "Master Robert was working for the King. He was doing his duty. It was so unfair. I have stayed here to restore the reputation and the good name of Catesby. We should not carry this shame just because the truth has been kept hidden. I've scoured Oxfordshire hoping someone would see me. Only now as I reached Northamptonshire have I found someone. You."

She started to cry. "You must help me, Mila. There is no-one else. I must clear Master Robert's name."

"I will help you, Mary, but Granny is calling me for lunch. Will you be here tomorrow?"

Wiping her eyes on a very fancy white handkerchief, Mary nodded.

Granny was standing at her open front door, waiting for Mila. In the afternoon, Mummy phoned to make sure she was alright. As the door was ajar, Mila could hear what Granny was saying but did not understand it.

"Yes, Olga, not naughty, no, but every time I looked outside to see what she was doing, she was sitting on the bench on her own. I told her to knock for Sienna but she didn't, just sat there, three hours, I think it was."

Mila was cross with Granny. What was she talking about? Mila had not been on her own. She had been talking to her new friend, Mary.

The next day was, again, a beautiful sunny day, just right for playing out. Mila wasted no time. She let Granny brush and plait her hair and was soon out of the door. She ran to the bench where Mary was waiting for her.

A little dog was barking but Mary was unconcerned. "Dogs don't like me and I don't like dogs."

Mila shooed the little dog away and was pleased when the dog did as it was told.

"Mary, what was it that you were saying about Mr James King? I must write to him and tell him to look into his records about a meeting. Is that right?"

"No, Mila, not Mr James King but King James. The one who is the head of the countries, England and Scotland…. Yes, write to him. Mila. What a lovely doll."

"Yes, she was a present from Granny. I've called her Caroline. Do you think that is the right name for her?"

The two girls turned their attention to the doll, strapping her in the new buggy.

Mila and Mary became firm friends during the week. On Friday it was time to say good-bye.

"Mila, you promise to send the letter?" Mary said.

"Yes, I will write but it is easier for me to do an email."

Mila saw Mary frown and so wanted to reassure her.

"It is nearly the same thing. Don't worry. Granny has promised to help me."

Mila had asked Granny about it so she was confident an email would be as good.

That afternoon, Granny was pleased Mila had asked her to help with an email. She didn't understand why Mila wanted to write it but it was enough her granddaughter wanted her help. The only suggestion Granny made was, the email should go to Queeen Elizabeth and not King James, explaining to Mila that the monarch had changed.

So Mila kept her promise to Mary and the next time she went to Granny's she looked for her. But she never saw her again.

Will Ye Choose to Live?

Pat Aitcheson

Going back to the past seemed strange to most people, but not Ben Vynall. Born to older parents who had given up hope of a child, he found adults easier to relate to than his peers. History fascinated him. He ignored the whispers and sneers of his schoolmates and carried on passionate discussions of battle tactics with his father during their visits to ancient monuments and battlefields.

Ben was lost when his parents died within six months of each other. For a time, he thought he might as well go the same way. But then he found his tribe in the historical re-enactment community. The Southland Company became the siblings and friends he never had. His weekends filled with purpose and the country fairs gave him something to talk about on Mondays in the County Surveyors office. Co-workers still thought he was odd, but he was used to it.

The Battle of Naseby was the most significant date in the re-enactment calendar. The Midland Festival planned to celebrate the 375th anniversary in some style, so Ben was unusually excited as he drove his van up the motorway from Sussex to Northampton on Friday. The fourteenth of June fell on a Saturday, the weather was fine and conditions couldn't be more perfect. Instead of cold mud, Southland Company would be setting up on dry fields for once.

Even better, he had a few days off afterwards to visit

some other historical sites. Ecton village was close by, where captured Royalist soldiers had been kept before marching the survivors to London for trial. Walking in the footsteps of those long gone gave him connection and a sense of his own place, at the end of a long line of forebears.

The convoy made excellent time and, before long, reached Whites Farm in Earls Barton.

Repetition had honed the company's skills in setting up camp. They split into groups and soon had both their living areas and the show tents ready. Ben was unfazed by superstitious talk about Friday the thirteenth; everything was working out well so far.

Some cooked their own food on campfires, laughing over a few beers. Others walked up the hill to the village for food and a pint at the Old Swan. Ben ate with his friends but declined alcohol, turning in early. He wanted to be well rested for the next day.

That night, he dreamed of long summer days, wheat fields harvest-ready and the unfamiliar, heady scent of hop fields, ripe for cutting. He woke in the dark, decided he shouldn't have eaten cheese before bed and fell asleep again.

Saturday morning dawned cool, with the clear blue sky promising more warmth later. Ben had a two-man tent to himself, which he preferred. He arranged his gear in meticulous order. Zipped plastic bags separated the different parts of his uniform. His maps were pristine, folded to show the area from Naseby to Ecton so he could orient himself properly. He checked his bandolier and musket again with care and then followed the smell of bacon.

He strolled over to Jack, who was camped next door. "Looks like a good day for it."

"It's early yet. Hope it doesn't get too hot, though." Jack flipped his rashers over. "I hate it when sweat runs down my back, ruins my jacket."

Ben nodded. Jack was better fed than most mediaeval villagers. The buttons on his jacket strained to contain his belly.

"You're right. Means more punters, though, so that's good for everyone. I can't wait to show them what we've got."

"Yeah. Local companies are arriving and we're on at eleven."

After breakfast, Ben joined the remainder of Southland Company for a final briefing. Theirs was one of thirty-two historical and re-enactment groups playing Royalists and Roundheads with cannons, horses, pikemen, muskets and infantry. They paraded on to the field to the sound of drums, wearing red jackets or sashes and bearing their lord's standards. Of course, a true battle was out of the question, but they charged and shouted, the cannons roared with fake charges and the crowd loved the spectacle.

After the battle, they manned the display tents to show how seventeenth-century people lived and worked. Ben's colleagues back in Sussex would hardly have recognised the lively enthusiast explaining the parts of the musket and demonstrating the firing process.

His proudest moment came when a mother thanked him for answering her son's many questions.

"Honestly, it's my pleasure," he said with a smile. "History is really about the ordinary man you know, pressed into service for a cause he didn't understand."

"Well, you did a great job with Adam. You listened and made him feel important and, yeah, you made history come alive for him."

"Thank you, and thank you, Adam."

The little boy waved and ran after his mother, leaving Ben with a smile that lasted all day.

It was a long, tiring Saturday but the best attended show any of them could remember. Despite sore feet and aching muscles, Ben and his friends were happy around their campfires. The sun sank below the horizon but the sky stayed light long afterwards as they talked and drank. Someone played a lute, its sweet sound a soft accompaniment to conversation.

Ben agreed to one beer, nursing it after it turned warm. He didn't care for the taste, but he'd learned to fake it since his father introduced him to real ale as a teenager. He was a grown man, after all.

"So, back to work on Monday, Ben?" Sarah's cheeks were flushed with sun and alcohol.

He shook his head. "Got some time off to visit a few local sites like Ecton and Naseby, and whatever else I can fit in."

"Good for you," she said. "I'd love to see more but got to whizz back on Sunday night. Real life calls, you know. Anyway, I'm turning in now. Tomorrow's another day and all that, besides I don't sleep that good on a camp bed."

"Night, see you tomorrow."

Sarah got up and stretched, then disappeared in search of her tent. Ben downed the last of his beer to be polite and said goodnight.

He woke to darkness and a full bladder. He cursed quietly. Why did he have that beer? Surely he was too young to have to pee in the night like his elderly father used to. He turned over and closed his eyes, hoping for sleep. Dreams came of angry skies and rain pelting unharvested crops, marching with cold rain in his boots and pungent clothes plastered to his body, dread heavy in his gut.

He bolted awake with his skin damp and crawling, afraid for a queasy moment he'd wet the bed. A quick check of his sleeping-bag reassured him. Light flashed outside. The forecast was good but perhaps a summer storm was brewing. It had certainly been hot enough. His bladder would not be denied any longer, so he pulled on his trainers and unzipped the tent door as another flash lit up the sky. He hurried to the toilet block, agitated without fully knowing why. The Portaloo smelled sour and stifling. He didn't delay.

"If it rains, it's not the end of the world," he muttered, unlocking the door.

Screams pierced the air, high-pitched and frantic, hardly human. A gust of wind blew the door wide open. A black horse galloped past, keening and bleeding with a pike trailing from its belly. Cannon thundered and a pall of smoke hung over a scrum of men and horses, bellowing and shouting and crying for mercy.

Ben gulped. His heart faltered in disbelief, then raced away, as if trying to escape his chest.

But he couldn't move.

The sky glowered down as men fought and died to the sound of the drum. In the endless melee, it was impossible to tell the sides apart. Some wore helmets, others hats, many had bare heads. Horsemen crashed among foot soldiers, slashing at them with swords dripping red.

A young man took a hoof direct to the face. The sound of his splintering skull carried clear to Ben's ears over the backdrop of combat. Soon the horse itself stumbled, a blade lodged in its guts. Its rider went down in a flurry of blows and screams. Men showed twisted, snarling faces red with fury, white with fear, blood their war paint.

Ben froze, his legs turned to stone. His guts liquefied and his hands shook. An acrid smell filled his lungs. He tasted copper and iron on the back of his tongue. Air thickened in his throat making each breath more difficult than the last. Some detached part of his brain mused that, if he had not already emptied his bladder, he would certainly have wet himself.

"Benjamin Vynall."

Words whispered in his ear turned his blood to ice.

"Benjamin Vynall. This be war, and here you lookin' like a rooster seen the axe."

He gasped, hyperventilating and shivering. In front of him, the battlefield faded to a distant roar behind a veil of fog.

"Here!" the voice slithered around him. "Open thine eyes."

A man appeared through the fog wearing a mud-splattered, faded red coat, a bandolier and a black hat with a feather. Ben's jaw dropped. He recognised the outfit, the musket, and the grimy face. Black eyes glittered in hollow sockets. Stringy dark hair clung to his dripping skull.

"Aye, d'you see me now? An' this rotten hellhole wherein I cower in fear of my life, on my Lord's whim?" His words creaked and groaned like a gate opened after many years.

Ben's mouth opened and shut. This could not be real.

His twin regarded him calmly. "Naught to say, Master Benjamin?"

Ben shook his head slowly. All the words curdled in his throat.

The soldier grinned, showing blackened irregular teeth. "This be war for the common man. We share a name but no fate. Would'st dwell here, in my stead, or no?"

The soldier's body jerked forwards as he took a hit. His grin stretched into a grimace. Blood spurted from his left thigh and he roared in pain, leaning on his musket for support. Then a passing rider swiped at his head and knocked him flat in the mud. Red burned in his eyes when he turned towards Ben.

"Around the globe, end o' the world," he gasped. His eyelids flickered shut and the battlefield faded into silent darkness.

Now able to move, Ben grabbed the open Portaloo door and slammed it shut. An icy trail of fearful sweat crept down his spine. After three tries, he managed to lock the door with shaky hands and sat on the closed toilet lid. A minute later, he leapt to his feet and vomited until green bile filled his mouth. He wiped his eyes.

"Only a dream. Only a dream." The whisper echoed around the tiny space. The smell was overwhelming. He needed a drink of water. There was a six-pack of bottled water in the tent. He was always careful to stay hydrated, especially in warm weather.

His mother's voice came to him. "Wouldn't want you getting sunstroke, Benji. That there sunstroke can be a nasty dose. Drink up now, there's a love."

Ben whispered to himself, "Only a dream." He unlocked the door.

A blow to the back of his head sent him reeling and he pitched face first into mud, seeing stars. He tried to sit up, but pain lanced hot through his left thigh and he cried out. His coat weighed him down and the bottles on his bandolier dug into his chest. Around him, battle raged. He blinked and gasped, starbursts of pain radiating through his leg. Something wet ran down his temple and cheek and he tasted blood on his lip.

The gunpowder. He had to get rid of the bandolier. If any of the bottles had broken, he'd be covered in gunpowder and that was not good.

Think. Focus.

Ben hauled himself to a sitting position. God, his leg hurt. He'd never known pain like it. Somehow the fight avoided him long enough for him to pull the bandolier off and toss it away. Only one bottle had broken, its jagged edges piercing his jacket and he saw red. Red on red, sticky on his palms.

Think, Benjamin. Focus.

He turned his head and saw bodies, limbs, horses,

discarded weapons strewn across the field. No green remained, only hoof-churned mud and blood and death. Pain overloaded his nerve endings and his vision faded into black. He shook his head.

Think.

All he had was his memory of the map. Up. He needed to go uphill, towards Earls Barton village. But where was he now? If he was west of his camp on Whites Farm, Ecton might be closer. Didn't matter.

Uphill. Start now.

He moved commando-style on his belly, away from the shouting and the flashes of cannon fire. Every part of his skin was wet. He rested for ten breaths at a time, no more. His thigh thrummed and sang with agony. He would have called it unbearable, except that would be saying he could not go on.

And he had to go on, up the hill, the pleasant walk he had planned transformed into a tortured journey. He had to go on because the alternative was to remain on the killing field, and he was not ready for death.

He crawled until the sounds faded and he could hear only his own rasping breath and moans. He had no idea how much time had passed. Daring to lift his head, he saw the inn standing alone, about two hundred yards away across the empty field. The windows were dark. Angry clouds swirled through the sky.

So he was at Ecton. Help was near.

Ben reached the back of the pub. He shivered, bone-numbingly cold all over, except for the hot stab in his leg with every movement. He sat up. There was no-one around, no houses, no birds. The sign creaked in the wind. He tried to get up, but his leg wouldn't hold him. He sat, head in hands, and cried.

He had not felt such isolated despair since the second funeral. On a bitter winter day, he'd dropped a handful of earth into his mother's grave and barely stopped himself from jumping in after it. Heart failure, the doctor told him. She woke up to find her husband cold next to her, dead of a massive stroke. Her future lost all meaning in that moment and she never got over it. An orphan not yet thirty, he was both too old and too young for his life. Grief almost drowned him, but he swam up from the depths until he could breathe again.

Think, Benjamin. Rally your forces.

His father's clipped tone sounded in his ear. Ben shuffled on his bottom to the oak front door and feebly banged on it. When no answer came, he moved to a window. There was a pile of old branches near the wall. He found a longer branch to use as a crutch and hauled himself to standing, gritting his teeth against the waves of pain. Then he hobbled around the building, knocking on every window and door.

"Help! Help, I'm hurt. Anybody help me?" Even to his own ears, he sounded weak and hoarse.

At the back of the inn, he glanced down the hill. For a moment, ranks of tents appeared. The groans of dying men filled his ears and the foul stench of gangrene wafted towards him. Bile rose in his throat. He blinked and was alone again.

He rounded the end of the inn and made his way back

to the road frontage. He glanced up at the picture of a globe on the sign as it swung and sighed above him. After one complete circuit with no answer, something broke inside him. He screamed and cursed at the top of his lungs and battered at the door with his fists, until he was dizzy and his hands throbbed. He collapsed on the ground.

"Master Benjamin."

He shook his head. There was no escaping this nightmare.

"Benjamin Vynall, when ye go around the globe, then ye reach end o' the world. And then 'tis time to be away home."

"I don't want this." The fight drained out of him. Everything hurt, even his thoughts.

"Would'st dwell here in my stead and share my fate or no? Will ye choose to live?" The voice broke off into racking coughs, wheezing and faint, until merciful darkness closed in.

Ben woke in his tent, drenched in sweat. He checked the time, only five o'clock. He pulled on his fleece and boots and walked out into the field. The morning was dry and fine. The camp slept and there was no sign of the torment he had endured.

He could almost believe it was a dream except his leg ached and the birthmark halfway up his thigh was tender as never before. When he lifted the hem of his shorts to check, he found the previously pale spot was raised, an angry red. He touched it gently and wondered if Sarah or one of the other women had any paracetamol. He'd never needed painkillers before. What the hell was happening to him?

Ben trudged over to his van, careful not to jar his left leg as he got in, and drove up to Ecton. There were a lot more buildings around as he pulled into a car park he had not noticed the night before.

The pub looked welcoming, with colourful hanging baskets outside. There was no traffic on the road at this hour. The village slept on. The World's End sign showed a person whose face was obscured by a helmet. He stood and looked up at the sign. His confusion only grew. What could he believe?

Only a dream.

He took part in Sunday's events feeling disconnected. He limped around the field, nausea gripping his gut, and flinched when the cannons fired. Real life seemed both more and less than before and he wondered whether he'd had too much sun after all. With past and present, fantasy and reality jumbled together, he was uncertain where he fitted in. He couldn't even confide in anyone. They'd take him away for sure.

That evening he returned to Ecton and got chatting to the barman about the pub's name.

"Was this pub always called The World's End?"

"Oh no, it used to be The Globe Inn. But after Naseby, when the losing Royalists were kept here, some were hanged and lots died of their wounds and that. It was the end of the world for them all right. And so the name changed."

"Interesting. That's why I'm here. For the festival. I came with one of the re-enactment groups." Ben sipped his lime and soda.

"Oh yeah, bringing history to life. I prefer the present day myself." The barman moved away to serve the next customer.

Monday morning, Ben sat in slow traffic on the road to Naseby. He had taken some of Sarah's paracetamols before setting off but kept rubbing his thigh. The clutch felt heavy, each press reminding him of the steady throb in the muscle.

The soldier's words rattled around his brain. Ben considered his options. What was he doing living in his parents' house, surrounded by the comforting detritus of their lives, spending his weekends as the youngest member of a group that immersed itself in the past? But when the others returned to their lives and families, he carried on looking back to a time that could never come again.

Maybe he could teach history instead. Adam and his mother had showed him there were other choices. The old house burdened him with its need for constant upkeep, though he'd made many happy memories there. Was that a life?

A blaring car horn pulled him out of his daydream, and he crawled forward ten yards. Ten miles from Naseby, he made a decision. Ben was not given to sudden changes of heart but, for the first time in his life, he listened to his gut. He pulled over and reset the satnav.

Back home, after taking another painkiller for his aching leg, he carefully unpacked his costume. He frowned as he examined the left trouser leg closely, tracing his finger over a frayed hole halfway up the thigh he didn't remember seeing when he packed it. The pocket bulged with something soft. He pulled it out. A handful of fragrant papery hops warm from the sun tumbled through his fingers.

"Will ye choose to live?"

That night he slept deeply with the hops under his pillow. Dreams came.

A man with Ben's face drank ale after a hot day in the fields, kissed a rosy-cheeked girl under an apple tree and never knew the horror of war.

And another man with the same face taught history with boundless enthusiasm to the faces of the future.

The Betrayal

James Dart

To look at the town of Northampton on that fateful day in the year 1645, one would be forgiven for believing that all was peaceful. Peasants worked in the fields, cobblers plied their trade, children ran about the street playing at amicable games. Closer inspection, however, would tell quite a different story. The eyes of the people were grey and drained as if their very souls had been torn from their beings.

For it was for their souls they feared. Thomas, a field worker, more than anyone else, was distraught and cursing his life. It was his children who had fallen ill. Elizabeth had been struck with fits first, then Mary and little Alan followed suit. They lay in their beds, shaking and convulsing like the recently slaughtered pig, sticky in their own defecations, as the carcase was in its own blood. First, concern swept the town, then fear, then panic as it slowly became evident what had caused this horror.

The devil himself had sent a representative. Witchcraft had infected Northampton.

The Witchfinder, one Matthew Hopkins by name, rode in with his devout followers on horseback. He extended hands to people on the street and they kissed them and backed away swiftly as though he were some rabid animal who may go berserk at any moment. This fear did not escape his notice. He withdrew his hands and stared forward, his jaw like a triggered bear trap. His work was unpopular but, as he intended to demonstrate, necessary. He would apply the full manner of his investigative skills to find this witch and they would see their errors and praise him like the saints and prophets of old. By God, they would.

* * * * *

Matthew Hopkins' followers came for Robert a few days later. He had returned home to find that his wife, Molly, was not there. He thought little of this, going for walks in the town being her custom, in which she often engaged in her favourite pastime of arguing with people. He had just begun working on the leather for a pair of boots when they kicked in the door and wrestled him from his seat.

They commanded him on to the back of a horse and the crowd averted their eyes, staring at the ground in silence, batting away tears of concern for their old and dear friend. They knew well he was being taken to the castle. They also knew very well why.

Robert himself was shaking almost as violently as the children of Thomas, his neighbour. He wept like a child as they brought him closer and closer to the place of his fate. He knew himself to be innocent but he also knew himself to be simple, simple enough that it would have been all too easy for a witch's sorcery to manipulate him. He prayed louder than he had ever done for God's forgiveness and for that of the Witchfinder. He was but a poor sheep who was not yet ready to face judgement from the Almighty and could not yet leave his beloved Molly.

"Mercy!" he cried. "O, mercy me!"

They dragged him, whimpering, through the castle, then down and down and down into the depths of the earth until he was sure he caught the taint of burning brimstone. He was pushed into a cold stone room. The door slammed behind him.

Sitting at the little wooden table in the centre of the room was a young man in priestly robes. He looked up at Robert with a kindly face which might have been sculpted from clay by God himself, two wide, gentle blue eyes regarding him almost lovingly as his mouth curved into a warm smile. Robert recognised him as the Witchfinder who had ridden into town some days ago.

"My son," the man said softly, gesturing to the stool on the other side of the table, "we have much to discuss."

Robert dropped to his knees next to the table, grasping at the man's robes. "Prithee, sir, you are a man of God, you must know that any part in the devil's grisly plan I may have played, I played it not willingly, or even knowingly. The Lord knows all, he must know this. I beg of you to spare me."

A hand caressed Robert's face and brought him up to look into the blue eyes once again. "Of course, my son. I am well aware you are innocent. You must forgive the brutish actions of my followers. They know all too well the importance of our task and they get somewhat enthusiastic. Sit down, have some wine."

Robert felt tears well up in his eyes. "Bless you, sir. Bless you." He slid on to the stool. With a shaking hand, he poured some of the wine into a goblet and threw it down his throat, tasting nothing but the burning in the back of his mouth. Burning away his sins and fears. He withdrew the goblet and gasped for air. "Anything I can do to help, I shall do."

The man smiled and nodded sagely. "I know well of your righteousness, as does the Lord. I merely need to ask you some questions. Are you ready to help in my Godly duties?"

"Yes sir."

"Of course. First, allow me to introduce myself, my name is Matthew. I was appointed by God to hunt down the servants of Satan who invade this realm." He leaned toward Robert, his blue eyes drawing him in. "What I am about to tell you may be hard to accept, it may even make you question your faith, but you must not falter. Are you ready?"

Robert was far from ready for such news. "Of course."

Matthew sighed, although his eyes stayed fixed on Robert's. It was now that Robert noticed the numerous scars on the man's face, too small to be seen from a distance, but obvious up close. Matthew placed his hand over Robert's arm in gentle support.

"Robert, your wife has confessed to being a witch."

Robert felt as if he had been impaled on a cold metal spike which shot through his stomach and heart. He sat, dumbfounded. "Good sir," he said, searching for the words which simply did not come. "There… there must be some mistake… "

Matthew sighed again. The deep and disappointed sigh of a sad father. "It is my duty to have her put to death, my son. Ordinarily, for defending her, you would go to the gallows along with her." He paused.

Robert grabbed his head with both hands, barely stopping himself from screaming.

Then Matthew held up a hand. "However, Satan masks his work well, my son. Is that not what you yourself said? You said that any role you played in his ploy, you played not willingly." He leaned forward, his gaunt chin pointing at Robert. "I believe you, my child! All you need do is do me the same kindness."

Doubt slowly writhed and pulsated across Robert's brain like fungi infecting the bark of a tree. He shrank in shame. He stared at the wooden table. "I apologise, sir. You are right about Satan's tricks." He looked up and stared into the man's pool-like eyes. "But you are mistaken of my Molly, sir. She is the Godliest and kindest woman I have ever encountered, of that I would swear before God himself."

"I am sure you would, my son," Matthew said with a falling expression. "I am sure you would." He straightened, as if he had been caught in the act of slouching by a superior. "You have attested to your wife's Godliness."

"I have and I would do so again one-thousand fold."

"I see. So, she is kind?"

"Yes."

"She does well by her husband?"

"Very well indeed, sir."

"She always goes to church?"

65

Robert hesitated. He was about to say yes again but something stopped him. It was not true. She did, sometimes, skip church of a Sunday. He put his hand to his temple. "She has good reason. She tends the field, she washes my clothes. There is much for her to do, as with any woman."

Matthew raised an eyebrow. "Yet other women manage to go to church each Sunday."

He was right. "Wha – What of it?" Robert said. "Many people do not go to church every week."

Another sigh. "Know you of what she does when you are at church?"

"Of course. As I said, she washes clothes, tends to the field… "

"And she does these things and nothing but these things while you are at church?"

Robert thought for a moment. "Perhaps she rests a little, eats some small morsels… " He wanted to say more. But the words died in his throat.

"Is it not possible – " Matthew said (The silence between his saying that and the completion of the question was, for Robert, like being trapped in a cage.), " – that your wife does other things? She is not being observed during that time. Did she not stay at home alone one Sunday before the children fell ill?"

Robert bit his lip. "I… I shall make sure my wife realises the error of her ways, sir, I swear it. Even if I have to beat her until she comes to church. Please understand, though, my wife being left home alone is of no consequence. Many would have had the opportunity to cast a spell. Indeed, there are many old crones who would have had ample opportunity as they live alone. They are widows, sir, they could be doing anything in their houses."

"Indeed," said Matthew.

Robert relaxed a little. Finally, he believed that he was on the way to making this man realise his mistake.

Then the Witchfinder spoke again. "Do any of these crones have a motive for making the children of Thomas and his wife ill?"

Robert shook his head. "I know not what you mean."

The Witchfinder sighed yet again. "Your wife is an argumentative woman, is she not?"

"Argumentative?" Robert said. "What do you – "

"She has made many a disagreement with several people in the town. I have many testimonies to this effect. Some even said they could see signs of the devil in her even then."

"Oh, dear sir," Robert said, "please, pay no mind to those people. Indeed, she is not well liked and I know that she is argumentative but… " The words would not come. "Pray, sir, from whom – "

Matthew put his hand up to silence him, his other hand drumming its fingers on the table. "Regardless of who, my child, the importance lies in the what. Your wife has had many quarrels with members of the community?"

Robert had to nod. "She can be bull-headed, true. But does this make her a witch?"

"Not on its own," Matthew said. "These disagreements, she has had several with Thomas and his wife, has she not?"

Robert gasped aloud. "Sir, I beg of you, understand – "

Matthew flattened his hands on the table. "Has she not?"

Staring at the table once again, Robert felt his heart being struck with icy, sharp agony. "She has, sir." His mind raced, each thought dragging him deeper into darkness. She skipped church, which not only meant that she had atheistic tendencies but also gave her opportunity. What was more, Thomas's stubbornness and her own gave her motive.

"How?" he muttered, grasping one final straw of hope. "How do you propose she did this?"

Matthew intertwined his fingers and leaned on his elbows. "You still have doubts? Very well, I suppose that is only natural. You are a good husband, my son, who has the utmost faith in his wife. However, your faith in God must be stronger. It must always be the strongest faith you have, the strongest love you have."

"It is," Robert said. "Please answer my question."

He nodded. "Witches' familiars are imps and low-ranking demons sent by Satan to relay instructions to his servants and help them to carry them out. They often take the form of cats or dogs. Your wife tends to cats, does she not?"

Robert's heart sank. "Yes."

"And was she not seen tending to this same cat in the days before the children became ill?"

"I do not know... but it is possible."

"More than possible, my child. Many have testified to it."

Robert was lost. His mind was nearly a complete blank.

He had been completely enveloped by dread and despair. His whole body went as limp as a fresh corpse. "Sir... may I speak to her?"

The Witchfinder let out his biggest sigh yet. "My child, you have been manipulated long enough. Besides, as I said, your wife has already confessed."

Robert sat still. Could he be right? If Robert had been manipulated by Satan, he would not have known. That was how Satan worked. Behind the curtain. While Molly had drawn him in and made him a puppet.

Dear Molly... she... was she really a witch?

Could he love a witch?

"Sir... please... "

Matthew stood and threw the table aside with a primal shout, Robert only just managing to avoid being hit. Robert shrank back as Matthew grabbed his clothing in tight fists and shook him hard, his teeth clenched and bared. "I am trying to save your soul from the eternal pit of Hell, Robert. Your wife is a witch. It has already been decided. Nothing can save her now, but you, you are different. You can be saved. You can be spared. The Lord's mercy is awe-inspiring, my child. You have a choice now. Accept His forgiveness, or stay ignorant and stay with your wife, with the witch who has played you for a fool for so long. Die choking for air and burn with her forever as rats gnaw on your scorched cheeks until they bite through and consume your tongue. It is your choice, my child."

Robert sank to his knees once again, tears in his eyes. "I wish to be saved, sir."

Matthew released him. He sat down on the other stool

and gave a harder sigh than Robert thought possible. "Then you will testify against your wife?"

"I shall."

Matthew's jaw softened and he grinned. He gave a satisfied grunt, which turned to a chuckle, which turned to full laughter. He held Robert's hand. "My child, you have made the right decision."

* * * * *

Robert testified against Molly at the courthouse.

The sympathy of the town was with him. They all commended him on his bravery and his Godliness. He no longer felt alone, no longer scrambling to make sense of it all. He was free of Satan's influence now. Free of Molly's manipulation.

After the verdict, Molly was taken to the gallows at Abington. All along the road, the people of Northampton shouted and pelted her with stones and rancid tomatoes. They were calling for her death and singing the praises of the Witchfinder General, Matthew Hopkins.

Robert walked behind the carriage, unwilling to look at Molly.

Thomas put a hand on Robert's shoulder. "I am glad that the Witchfinder was able to free you from Satan's power. Many in town thought him but a charlatan and a fingerman, but he proved them all wrong. He got his witch and saved the innocent. Worry not, my friend. This will all be over soon. Both your suffering and mine."

The gallows were already set up on their arrival. Molly

begged, tried to cast her spell, but it was too late. The executioner stood her before the crowd and for the first time since he had last seen her, before he knew the truth, Robert looked at her face and it shook him to his core. She was terrified.

The executioner approached her with a sack. Her eyes danced around the crowd, trying to find someone to bewitch. Finally, with a freezing bolt through his being, their eyes met. She said nothing, her eyes pleading with him. Her head was then covered.

Robert covered his face with his hands. Another second and he would have been bewitched yet again.

He could not bear to look. After what seemed like days, he heard the sound of the trap door opening, followed by a deafening, blood-curdling snap, the roar of the crowd and, finally, it was over.

Robert uncovered his eyes. He was still shaking but, slowly, surely, his fear lifted. He would be manipulated no longer.

Shelter from the Storm

Chris Wright

As the first flakes of snow fell, Martha hurried across the courtyard of Kirby Hall. Reaching the lobby, she slowed and took the broad, winding staircase, ignoring the detritus scattered across the floor and the broken plaster on the walls. She imagined herself an Elizabethan lady, some three centuries before, leaving a feast in the Great Hall and returning to the luxury of her rooms.

At the top of the stairs, she glanced left to the Long Gallery, stifling a shudder. Long shadows from the absent roof stretched across the decaying, hole-riddled floor.

She turned right to the Great Chamber. A few tattered pieces of wallpaper hung from the walls, illuminated by the low sun. Much of the floor was in darkness, making it harder to pick her way amongst the scattered wood and masonry. It only took a little care, though; it was a path she had trodden countless times.

She reached the bedchambers and approached the bay windows. Once, it had been a view reserved for lords and kings. Now, it was just a vantage point across to the other side of the brook. She could just make out her father, brother and the two dogs bringing a handful of sheep back towards the house. The grass below was already disappearing beneath a carpet of white, but Papa and William would be safely indoors before it became treacherous.

She turned the iron latch and pushed the window open.

"Papa!" she called, waving to try and catch his attention. "Papa!"

After a moment he waved back. Martha was content he would know the stew was ready and would make his way home. Martha returned to the courtyard, the chill of the cold wind making her shiver as she crossed it again. Covered in a thin coating of snow, she arrived back at the rooms they called home. It was coming down heavier now.

Martha pumped water into a large copper pot and put it on to the range to heat. It was nearly boiled by the time Papa and William returned, stamping their feet on the stone of the kitchen.

"Did you gather all the flock?" she said.

"We're still missing two." Papa hung his coat. "It's going to be bad tonight. We'll search in the morning, but I fear we'll lose them."

Once the stew was served, they ate and told each other of their days. There was little new to tell so, once the dishes were cleared, they settled down and listened to William read from a chapbook he'd recently bought. He could read better than Papa or Martha. He made the words come to life and it was easy to picture the tale they described. The hairs on Martha's arm stood up as Robinson Crusoe discovered a man's footprint and then human bones from a cannibal's feast.

All too soon, William was yawning and putting the book to one side while Papa dozed in his armchair.

"Oh, don't stop now," she said. "I want to know if

Robinson and Friday rescue those two men."

William smiled. "You'll have me reading till after midnight. We'd be no use to anyone in the morning."

"But don't you want to know what happens? Or go to sea and have an adventure yourself?"

"Of course I do. I'd love to be out there doing something exciting." He picked the chapbook up again. "But this isn't real life; it's just a way to escape."

"Can you really imagine living like this forever? I don't think I can."

"It's the way it is for the likes of us." William put the book down again. "Our life isn't a bad one, living in a fine house – "

"A ruin," Martha corrected.

"But what a ruin! And we've got Alice... you can't pretend she's ordinary or boring."

"You shouldn't say her name, William. She – "

" – can hear us? We've no reason to think that."

"That's enough of that talk, both of you."

Martha jumped. Papa was wide awake, frowning. "It's time we took to our beds. There's still sheep to find in the morning."

Martha bade them goodnight and went upstairs to her room overlooking the courtyard. As she closed her curtains, she looked out. The snow was still falling, swirling in a strong wind and making a thick blanket of white on every surface.

She awoke in the night to the sound of the sheep stirring outside. Martha turned in her bed and settled. The sheep bleated again and she rose, pulling back the curtain. The flock had clustered on the near side of the courtyard. Across, on the opposite side, a glow of blue light filtered through the upper windows of the Long Gallery. The missing roof and decaying floor allowed her to see it through the lower windows and doors and against the still standing chimney breasts.

Martha let the curtain drop.

It was Alice.

She'd told William not to say her name.

She pulled the curtain again to make the smallest gap. The light began to move and there Alice was, at one of the large windows. The form of a young servant girl, dressed in old-fashioned garb, moving slowly along the gallery. The movement was too smooth to be a walk, and Martha knew there was no floor in the place. Alice passed out of view, appearing again in the next window. The pace increased and the reflected glow began to move rapidly until she reached the final window, almost opposite Martha's own.

There the apparition came to a halt, in full view. Martha could make out the profile of the face, a young woman, pretty with prominent cheek bones. The far wall was visible through her. Martha realised she wasn't breathing and took in a gulp of air.

Alice stood motionless for an age, then turned and looked directly at Martha.

Martha was transfixed.

Finally, shaking, she let the curtain fall into place and stepped back from her window. Cold sweat trickled down her face and the arch of her back. Alice haunted the Long Gallery – there'd never been any tale of her going beyond.

She shouldn't be able to come to this side of the courtyard.

Martha returned to her bed, pulling the covers over her. She told herself again and again that nothing could happen. But every creak of a floorboard, every movement of the sheep outside, became a harbinger of ghostly menace.

There was a noise outside in the hallway, the sound of her doorknob being tested. She froze, holding her breath. The knob turned and the hinges creaked as the door opened. She stifled a near overwhelming instinct to scream.

"Martha... " a voice whispered. It was William. "Are you all right?"

She pushed her bed covers back, hurried to William, hugged him. After a moment, she felt his arms enfold her, strong, safe.

"You're shaking," he said. "Did you have a nightmare?"

"It's Alice," Martha sobbed. "She's there. She looked right at me."

William released her and went to the window, pulling the curtains open. "It's all right. There's nothing there now. See?"

Martha glanced through. It was as he'd said, Alice was gone.

William gave her another hug and guided her back to bed.

"We shouldn't have spoken of her," Martha said as he turned to go.

He opened his mouth to respond then nodded. "Try to get some sleep."

Martha did her best, but sleep eluded her.

In the morning, she rose with the first light and set

about her chores. William seemed to be more attentive than normal but said nothing about the night's events. When they had breakfasted, he and Papa put on their warmest clothing and left to search for the last two sheep.

An icy draught entered the kitchen as they opened the door. The snow was piled up a good two feet across the doorway and they had to clear it with shovels before they could be on their way.

Papa surveyed the state of the courtyard. "Doesn't look good. I'm not sure how long it'll take, but we'll be back before dark, whatever happens."

Martha busied herself, baking bread, clearing some more snow from around their doorway and putting extra hay out for the flock.

Not long after noon, she heard William call her name from outside the house. She hurried to the courtyard entrance to see Papa and him carrying a man between them. The man wasn't moving, and they were struggling under the burden to find their footing in the snow.

"We found him over near the road," Papa called. "He must have got lost in the storm."

"Is he dead?" Martha said.

"He's not far off. Get hot water on, as many blankets as you can find… and ready William's bed."

Martha hurried back to their rooms, putting water on the range and searching the cupboards for all the blankets she could find.

By the time Papa and William arrived, all was ready. The man was wrapped too thinly against the cold and his skin was white. Martha put a hand to his forehead; it was far too cold and his clothes were sodden from the snow.

"Take him upstairs and dress him in a nightshirt. There are blankets there already. I'll be up when he's decent."

Papa and William struggled to get the man up the stairs and, once they'd managed it, there were a succession of loud clatters as they attempted to get him changed. There were some tasks that men just seemed to find difficult.

As the noise quieted, Martha filled two foot warmers with hot water and carried them up. The door was open; the man was under the covers of the bed. She wrapped the foot warmers in cloth and placed them either side of his torso.

"There's little we can do now but wait," Papa said. "See if we found him soon enough."

"I'll sit with him," Martha said. "You go and find the sheep."

After they left, she took up a pan of hot water and rested a warm damp cloth on the man's forehead. His breathing was shallow at first, but slowly it eased and colour returned to his skin. He was young, not long in his twenties, Martha judged, and, despite an unfashionable growth of beard, he was handsome. His hands were too soft for a labourer but his face was weathered.

Once she was certain the man would not expire, she took his clothes downstairs and washed them. They were good quality, though simple in style. Emptying the pockets, she found letters tied together with string, a few shilling coins and folded bank notes. There must have been near ten pounds in total. She put everything safely in a drawer.

What manner of man had they found?

He showed no sign of waking, so Martha continued with her routine. Just before dark, Papa and William returned. They had found only one of the sheep, caught in brambles and frozen to death. Papa had lost two of the flock, something they could ill afford.

As they were eating, they heard a noise upstairs – the man calling, though his voice was weak. All three rushed to William's room. The man was trying to push himself up, with little success.

"Rest," Papa said. "You'll need time to recover."

"Where am I?" the man asked. His accent was strange. Martha had never heard the like of it.

"You're in Kirby Hall, son, or what's left of it. We found you out in the snow. You're lucky to be with us. What's your name?"

"Ezekiel, sir. Ezekiel Braithwaite."

"I'll fetch some sweet tea and broth," Martha said. "You must be hungry."

"Aye, I am at that," Ezekiel replied with a weak smile. "Famished."

She brought them up a few minutes later. William had helped Ezekiel to a sitting position, and Martha handed him the tea. Ezekiel tried to lift the cup to his lips, but it started to shake and almost spilt.

Martha steadied the cup in his hands and took the weight. "Here, let me." She tipped the cup to his lips and he took a small sip.

"Look at me," he said. "Like a babe in arms."

Martha helped him with the broth, raising the spoon to his mouth. When he was done, Ezekiel settled back, propped against the head of the bed and almost immediately his eyes became heavy.

"We should leave him to rest, Papa, and not crowd him so."

"He speaks so strangely," Martha said back in the kitchen. "It's not easy to understand what he says."

"He must be from the north," William replied. "And what sort of name is Ezekiel?"

"A good Bible name," Papa said, "and he's from Lancashire. There was a chapman who used to come round when you were children who spoke just like him. He's a long way from home."

It snowed again that night and on into the following day, Friday. Papa and William would usually have gone to the market in Corby. The deep snow and the unexpected visitor meant that would have to wait.

Ezekiel slept most of that morning as well. Martha took some food up to him around noon and sat at the bottom of the bed while he ate.

"Papa says that you're from Lancashire."

"Aye, Blackburn." He grinned at Martha. "What gave it away?"

"Your accent is – oh!" Martha felt herself blushing and lowered her gaze. "You're teasing me."

"I'll have to do it again. You have a pretty smile."

Martha coloured even more and tried to change the subject. "Why were you out in the storm? You could have died."

"That I could," Ezekiel replied, "and I'm grateful to you all for your help. I'd decided last year to go to London and find my way there. I've been chompin' at the bit all winter and wanted to get started. Looks like I left a bit too early."

Martha thought of the money she'd found. "Was your life so terrible?"

"Terrible? No... I'd not say that. But it was all mapped out for me. My father's overseer at t'cotton mill and my brother, Isaiah, and I were to follow him."

"That sounds like a good life."

"Aye, I'd not want for money. Isaiah'll take my father's job one day, but there are plenty of mills and I'd have found a place of my own, with t'same owners, most like."

"So why leave?"

"I just wanted something... more. To be my own man. I've always loved that story about Dick Whittington. I'm going to do the same, make my own fortune."

"Oh yes. That's one of my favourites, too." Martha smiled. "I often get William to read that for us of an evening. The book is dog-eared now and I think he's fed up with it."

"So, you have your dreams too, Martha?"

She nodded. "Yes, but that's all they are."

Martha found herself drawn to the stranger with his exotic accent. Over the next few days, as his strength returned and the slowly melting snow prevented Papa and William from doing much outdoors, she and William spent time with Ezekiel, listening to his plans.

He would attach himself to a fine gentleman, become his right-hand man. Or perhaps he'd go on a sea voyage and make his fortune like Dick Whittington. Or he'd set up his own business buying and selling goods from the East Indies.

It sounded so exciting, though William was less impressed.

"Ezekiel's a dreamer," he said when they were alone. "His plans are half-baked."

"You're just jealous. He's going to make something of his life."

"Perhaps... perhaps not. If he wants to go to sea, why's he going all the way to London? There's a perfectly good port right near him at Liverpool. There's something more to his story, or does he really believe the streets are paved with gold in London?"

William was being a stick in the mud. What was so wrong about having dreams?

As the snow cleared, Papa decided he would go to Corby market on Tuesday and take Ezekiel there on the cart.

Papa and William spent Monday getting the sheep back out into the pasture, so Martha gave Ezekiel a tour of her extended home.

"This is amazing," he said as they walked through the Great Chamber, looking out on to the grounds outside. "You're lucky to live here."

Martha touched a peeling strip of grimy wallpaper. "It's just a ruin now."

"But you can almost see the lords and ladies who used to walk these rooms. Just imagine being one of them." He gave an elaborate bow.

Martha giggled and curtsied. "Oh, I do. It's what makes this place bearable."

Ezekiel held out his hand. "Come, my lady. Let us continue our tour."

Martha placed her hand upon his, the way she imagined a lady would, and they walked on.

Ezekiel stopped and turned towards her. He raised her hand to his lips and kissed it gently. "Come with me, Martha. Come to London."

"What?"

"We're the same. We don't want to stay trapped in lives chosen for us. Just think what we could do together."

"I couldn't... What would Papa do without me?"

"He'd manage... He can't expect you to stay forever. Think about it, at least."

Martha nodded, unsure what to say.

Ezekiel led her onwards. "Who knows, we might even have a great house of our own one day. With servants who would – "

"Stop!" Martha said.

They had reached the top of the stairs and Ezekiel had been walking on towards the Long Gallery.

"Why?" he asked. "The floor looks safe for a good way yet."

Martha took her hand from his. "We... we don't go down there. It's haunted."

"Haunted?" Ezekiel looked more intently down the length of the ramshackle room. "Are you serious?"

"It's – " Martha caught herself before she said Alice's name aloud. "A servant girl... from hundreds of years ago. She died in this room, raped and killed by the son of a visiting lord. She's haunted this place ever since. They say that if she touches a person, their heart stops in an instant."

Ezekiel laughed, though he took a step backward as he

did so. "You're kidding me. A joke you play on your visitors."

Martha shook her head. "I'm not joking. I've seen her myself... several times. My room looks across the courtyard."

"I don't believe in ghosts."

"Well, you'd change your mind if you'd seen what I have."

Martha led him downstairs.

That night, sleep didn't come quickly for Martha. Ezekiel's proposal dominated her thoughts. It could answer her dreams with a life beyond Kirby Hall and sheep farming. But was William right? Was Ezekiel a dreamer headed for poverty? Or was this the best chance she would ever have? Her thoughts circled round and round till eventually she slept.

The next morning, as Papa and William prepared the horse and cart, Ezekiel came downstairs, dressed once more in his own clothes.

"Have you thought about my offer?"

"I've done nothing else."

Ezekiel approached and put his hands on the side of her shoulders. "Will you come?"

Martha shook her head and took a step away from him. "No. My place is here."

"I know you want to. You're just too scared to take the first step out of the door."

"Partly," Martha admitted. "But I realised I have a lot here too."

Papa's footsteps echoed on the stone outside, and the

85

door opened. "We're ready to go, Ezekiel. We ought to make a start."

"Then this is goodbye."

Ezekiel turned and left, following Papa out to the cart. Martha watched them go from the doorway. She had done the right thing... she hoped.

With the men away, it was a busy day. She had her own tasks to attend to as well as checking on the flock. She started cooking later than normal, as she knew Papa and William would not be back from Corby until after dark.

While she was peeling turnips, she felt a rush of cold air, turned and let out an involuntary gasp. Ezekiel stood there, already in the kitchen.

"You made me jump. But why... why are you here?"

He smiled. "Why do you think? I'm here for you. I knew you couldn't say what you really felt with your father close. So, I came back."

"Oh Ezekiel... you've had a wasted trip. I meant it. I'm going to stay here."

He moved forward, putting his arm around her waist and pulling her close. "I know you like me, that you want more. This is your chance." He leaned forward and kissed her.

Martha pushed against him as hard as she could, partly freeing herself. "No! Get off me." She raised her right hand, still holding the peeling knife. "Please... go."

His face changed, cheeks colouring. "Don't you threaten me, you tuppenny whore. You're all the same, promising everything, then leaving a man dangling."

Ezekiel took a step forward and, despite the knife,

Martha took a step back. His left arm moved in a flash and before Martha could react, he had a hold of her wrist, squeezing it until the knife dropped from her grasp.

Martha kicked hard at his shin. Screaming in pain, he released her arm to nurse his leg. She took her chance, running past him and out through the doorway.

"You bitch! You'll pay for that."

Martha raced across the courtyard and into the lobby. She looked back to see Ezekiel leaving the kitchen, limping but still mobile. She hurried through the downstairs rooms to the lower bedchambers. The gloom was growing, but she could see back through to the lobby. She waited for Ezekiel to appear.

Making sure he had seen her, Martha moved swiftly to the adjoining bedchamber, then beyond to some servants stairs she had not shown him. He would follow, allowing her to double back on the upper floor, then use the main stairs to escape. His injured shin would slow him.

She made her way through the upper rooms, starting to breathe heavily from the exertion. She reached the top of the stairs at a run and prepared to descend.

There he was, almost at the top of the stairs.

Martha tried to stop but her momentum carried her on, clipping the corner of the far wall with her shoulder. She cried out and stumbled, spinning as she struggled to regain her balance.

She stood, trembling, Ezekiel to her front and the Long Gallery to her back.

Tears welled in Martha's eyes. "Let me go, please."

"Aye, I will… when I'm done with you."

Martha tried to run past him, but he caught her and pushed her backward. She lost her footing and fell to the floor.

"Alice!" Martha called out loudly. "Alice!"

Ezekiel stood over her and slapped her across the face, making her cheek and the side of her head burn hot.

"Quiet!"

Martha whimpered. "Alice," she called again, but the power of her voice was gone.

Ezekiel lifted his hand a second time. Martha raised her arms protectively, but the blow never came.

A soft blue light bathed the area.

Ezekiel looked up, then to Martha. "It's real?"

Martha rolled on to her side so she could see. A hundred feet along the gallery, Alice hovered a few inches above the broken floor. She was coming towards them at a sprint, though her legs never moved.

Ezekiel backed away a couple of steps, then turned to run. The gloom descended again as Alice was gone. A moment later she was standing right in front of Ezekiel at the top of the stairs.

He let out a shriek, turned again to run past Martha and into the gallery, floorboards creaking as he did so. Ten strides in, the floor gave way and he disappeared from sight, screaming.

Martha stood and edged closer to look over the newly created edge. Ezekiel lay crumpled like a rag doll, bleeding heavily from a wound to his head.

The blue glow filled the room and Martha realised Alice was only a couple of feet from her.

As their eyes met, a smile flickered at the edge of Alice's mouth. She moved away, slowed, turned and came close once more. Still smiling, Alice reached out, enfolding Martha in an incorporeal embrace.

Martha struggled. "No. Wait!"

"You are safe, now."

Blackness closed in on Martha's mind, consuming her.

Part 2: Contemporary Stories

The Biddenham Ghosts

Deborah Bromley

In the depths of the countryside, away from the ochre glow of urban streetlights, darkness settles on the landscape like a black shroud on a corpse. Pavements shift and become insubstantial, buildings hug the land, seeking the solid earth to guard themselves from night-time uncertainties. Trees creak and sway as the wind gusts through their branches. Skies gather their clouds and blanket everything with gloom. A waning crescent moon reveals unlikely shadows as the clouds part and close up again.

The night bustles with nocturnal creatures. A fox, sprightly after a blood-soaked feast, trots replete across the field to its lair. A Muntjac deer barks for its mate, then creeps deeper into the woodland to wait. A field mouse, nimble and silent, scampers up to the bird table, huddling to avoid the piercing talons of the owl as it swoops towards the oak trees. Two cats, locked in a stand-off, fur raised, bodies arched, back away and run towards their homes and the prospect of a warm bed by the fire.

The pub, The Three Casks, turns out its reluctant regulars and the landlord drapes towels over the pumps. The door is locked and the lights are extinguished. His wife calls him up to their cosy apartment and he sets the intruder alarm before he ascends the stairs. Two gentlemen douse their final cigarettes, plunging them into the sand bucket by the door, before muttering farewells and walking, unsteadily into the night.

This is an ordinary night. The darkness and the sounds of its natural inhabitants provide familiarity and comfort. Behind the floral curtains of cottages and barns, villagers bank up the Aga, stir mugs of Horlicks or settle on a well-deserved tot of rum to send them off to the land of Nod. Or up the stairs to Bedfordshire, as they aptly repeat, whenever the fancy takes them.

The village road curves around wide verges, then bisects a triangle of green space that houses the village sign, before disappearing towards the church or veering away to the main road. Dusk Cottage, nestled under a thickly thatched roof, secured by an arched oak door, strong with black rivets, looks out over the green space. An estate agent's board announces it is "For Sale". Empty rooms lie behind the thin curtains. Cold grates wait for a new owner to light a fire.

Away to the right, a hand-painted sign announces the path to the village pond. The path is known as Coffin Path, the most direct route from the old village morgue which is located in the gardens of The Three Casks, towards the church and the chance of a proper Christian burial. When sturdy men would carry the deceased the half-mile towards St James, the shortest path was always preferred.

Coffin Path is dark and empty. Recent rain has made the nettles surge and muddy paw and foot prints trace it towards the silent pond where it creeps further into the night and away towards its final resting place in the churchyard. As if on cue, the church bell sounds eleven o'clock.

Dusk Cottage stands foursquare on its plot, its foundations of brine-soaked ship's timbers bracing the frame and bonding it with the bare earth it stands on. Yet, if you look closely enough and know what to look for, you'll notice a loose copper strip dangling by the front door, disconnected from the thick copper spike in the dark soil. If you understand the meaning of this damage, you will knot your brows and wonder about the consequences. But that requires a deeper understanding, a sense of the natural order of earth, water, fire and air, of the energy that criss-crosses the land and transmits a signal to those who can sense it. You'll know then that the balance has been upset. Energy that should flow towards other villages, towards other intersections, flow unhindered towards centres of great significance, that ancient energy that you understand now pools, brooding and spiteful around the mouth of Coffin Path.

"Who is that walking by the War Memorial? Do you know them?"

"Where? Actually, is there anybody there? I can't see anybody."

"You're right. It's the odd light at this time of day. I have seen a strange woman hanging around, though. Definitely not someone I recognise from the village."

"I think I know who you mean. She said hello to me the other day at the post box. Her family have just moved into

The Old Vicarage."

"How interesting."

"And she's not strange. Quite normal and friendly. The family have moved here from abroad somewhere, I'm not quite sure where. They have two children and her name is Kate."

"Mystery solved, then."

"I wouldn't want to live in that house."

"Me neither. It depends on whether or not you can see dead people, I suppose."

"I'm told it's much worse if you can feel them. More creepy."

"Well, let's face it, in this village, you get plenty of opportunity for both."

"Let's turn around at the bus shelter, I don't feel like going to the pond tonight."

"Fine. Let's get these dogs home before it gets dark."

Sophie puts her sandwich down on the side table and turns on the television. She has some programmes recorded her dad thinks are rubbish. If she doesn't watch them when she has the chance, he'll delete them. She settles down to watch Paranormal Lockdown. In this episode, the investigators will be locked in a long-disused mental hospital for 72 hours.

The dogs barge through the lounge door and settle alongside her on the sofa. They will do anything for food and believe the last bits of a sandwich crust are theirs by right.

"There, eat up and that's your lot. Now you can get down. Go on, get down both of you."

Charlie ignores her and sneaks away to snuggle under a cushion but Ollie obediently gets down and takes up his normal position by the front window.

Sophie thinks about getting up to close the curtains and block out the night but can't be bothered. The front patio windows look out over a small enclosed garden with its honey stone paving and ivy-covered stone wall. Although it's pitch dark outside and the blackness makes the room less cosy, she needs early warning of her parents return so she can get out her schoolbooks and pretend she's been revising. From where she sits, any car headlights coming towards the house will be visible. She clicks play on her recording. Charlie starts to snore loudly. She turns the volume up. Ollie twitches in his sleep.

On the television, the lockdown is in progress and the team are bedding down in the operating theatre. That's where they expect to get the most paranormal activity. They have already set up night vision cameras, electronic voice recorders and electromagnetic detection devices. So far, so normal. They also have a spirit box, but not just any old spirit box. They are testing a new device, designed by one of the technicians, that projects magnetic resonance in lines forming a grid the size of the human body. The theory is that a dead person could use the energy to manifest inside it. During the set-up, the gridwork lights up the room in spooky blues and greens, casting strangely shaped shadows on the walls and ceiling. Then there's the unbelievable noise. The manic hum, the crackling, the bangs and thumps.

"'Holy shit, it's already picking something up," one of the presenters says.

"Step away from it. The energy is building."

"What's that? Did you touch me?"

"God, I felt that, too."

Then the power goes off and the television blacks out and all Sophie can see is the faint outlines of the furniture. She is seriously annoyed and she sits for a while, hoping it will come back on again. She wonders when her parents will come back, then tries to remember where the fuse box is located and what she should do to get the power back on.

"'You are so not helping," she says to the dogs.

Neither dog seems bothered by the darkness. Sophie crawls off the sofa and crouches down at the fireplace. Her hand finds one of the scented candles. She fumbles in the log basket and locates the box of matches. Striking the match and lighting the candle, she sits back on her haunches, feeling pleased she's done something useful. She then lights the other two candles.

"Cosy. Now what do we do, dogs? Come on. Let's find my phone."

Upstairs, the floorboards creak.

"No way."

She looks down at the floor and sees Ollie has raised his head off the carpet. Charlie is still buried under a cushion. The creaking continues. Her voice dies in her throat. Not ordinary, *heating coming on* type creaking, but more like *person walking slowly on the upstairs landing* creaking. She stops breathing. The top step squeaks. It always does. She realises she knows exactly how every footstep sounds in this old house. This noise is of somebody or something coming down the stairs.

Ollie sits up, his head cocked to one side in the candlelight. She sees his lips curl back, revealing his large, white teeth. A low rumble sounds in his chest.

Still she can't breathe.

Then the lights flash back on and the telephone bleeps and the television comes back on and Ollie stares at the lounge door, his hackles stiff and his body hunched, ready to pounce.

That's when she screams.

"Did you get a power cut last night?"

"No."

"Well, we did, it seems. Sophie was totally freaked out by the time I came home, saying something about noises on the stairs."

"Sounds scary."

"Not what you need when the electricity goes off."

"Is she all right?"

"Yes, back to normal but we had to spend some time reassuring her. We walked up and down the stairs and across the landing a few times. Nothing like the noises she heard, apparently. I think it was just a coincidence that the heating pipes were cooling down or heating up when the power went off."

"Our house creaks all the time and it's only five years old."

"How far shall we go today?"

"Let's go by the side road on to the golf course. Give the dogs a nice run."

Sophie lies in bed looking at the shadows on the ceiling, thinking about how frightened she was when the power went off. She can hear the familiar murmur of her parents talking downstairs, making a drink, putting the dogs to bed. Then she thinks about Ollie and how terrified he was. She has never seen him like that. Her heart speeds up and she has to concentrate on her breathing to get herself calmed down. She pulls the duvet closer and tucks her nose under the covers. She hears the front door being locked and the downstairs lights being switched off. The glow from her bedroom doorway is suddenly dimmed.

"Night, darling."

"Night, Mum, Dad."

"See you in the morning."

Sleep blurs the senses and makes reality seem insubstantial. Sophie wakes in the night, her feet tangled up inside the duvet. The house is quiet. She reaches down and tugs the cover away. Then she notices it. On the right of her bed. A weight, pressing down, a dead weight. As if somebody is sitting on the side. Or maybe a dog. But Ollie and Charlie are in the kitchen, she knows that for certain.

"Mum," she whispers. Or maybe she just thought it in her head, she can't tell because her heart is thumping so loud the noise is deafening.

She daren't move.

She daren't breathe.

She daren't think.

Then it happens. The weight lifts. There's a muffled sound of footsteps, soft on her carpet, padding softly in the direction of her wardrobe. Then nothing.

This time she finds she can't scream.

"I met that woman Kate today, the one I told you about. Really nice lady. She's putting both her girls into the village school after half-term."

"Good, that'll boost the numbers."

"Found out some interesting things about the house. Things even I didn't know."

"Well?"

"It seems they did some in-depth research before they decided to buy it. When it was the actual rectory, apparently they buried the stillborn babies in the garden. There are loads, like from when everyone suffered with infant mortality."

"I hope there aren't any dead babies in our garden."

"But your house is a barn so there will only be dead sheep or pigs or whatever."

"Thank you for pointing that out."

"That's just how it is. She told me one of the rectors lost about eleven or twelve children. Really sad. The stillborns weren't allowed to be buried in the churchyard as they hadn't been baptised."

"That is very sad, seems quite unChristian by today's standards."

"Little lost souls, so many little lost souls."

101

Darkness plays on your mind when you are afraid. There are no streetlights in this part of the village. People boast about how they prefer the darkness. No light pollution cluttering up the sky and interfering with the stars. How Sophie longs for some comforting streetlights.

It's another evening at home. Another chance to watch a recorded programme while her mother is at a committee meeting and her father is having a drink at the pub. Both of them only five minutes away. But the darkness doesn't know or care as it creeps closer.

The creaking – she is used to it. It can't be explained but she's used to it. The night terrors are not so easy to explain. She doesn't broach the subject with her parents. She can't make the words come out of her mouth. To do that will make it real. Once the words have been said, they cannot be taken back. Anyway, what can anyone do?

She invites the dogs on to the sofa and cuddles them close, bribing them with a digestive biscuit. Then she puts on the extra light by the sideboard and wills herself to calm down. The television is turned up loud, loud enough to drown out any sounds she doesn't want to hear. The dogs are her barometer. She strokes them and checks that they are relaxed. She has shut the curtains but doesn't feel safer. The room feels closed in, claustrophobic, so she opens them again.

Ollie lays across her lap, dribbling on to her sleeve. The television show plays out on the screen, the flashing lights reflected faintly in the window. Something catches her eye through the patio window, a head and shoulders moving in her peripheral vision above the front stone wall. She dismisses it as one of the neighbours' children or a family friend. A pale blonde blur of hair moving above the stone garden wall, disembodied. The dog snores and twitches, unimpressed.

She concentrates on the programme. She has to concentrate on the programme. The flash of lights, the canned laughter, the inane presenting. Then she hears the sound of a car. A door slams. The bleep of a remote control. Her mother's head appears over the wall and she waves. Her mother's head, visible and lit up by the security light on the drive. Clear and crisp and real.

She looks at the front patio window and notices again how the television screen is reflected on the right side. And then a shutter snaps open inside her head. A deep, knowing part of her understands that the pale head she had seen earlier had not been outside the room, walking in the road in front of the garden wall. Her skin begins to crawl. She forces herself to look to the right, past the book cases, towards the back wall with the mirror. And she realises that what she had seen was the reflection of a disembodied head walking from one side of the living room to the other.

Sophie waits in the darkness for the arrival of the weight on her bed, the silent, brooding weight. She is powerless to stop it happening. It is now her secret. She cannot explain it or speak about it.

Inside the cocoon of her bed, she listens for the other sounds, the ones she now knows will follow. The creak of the floorboard outside her bedroom door. The swish, as if the hem of a silky dress is dragging along the carpet. The sudden tap of an invisible knuckle on her wardrobe door. Then the padding footfalls inside her room. The inescapable knowledge that she is being watched. There is no shock, not like in the films or the programmes she used to love so much. Just the horrifying inevitability that soon, one night very soon, whatever is in the room will come for her.

By Coffin Path, the darkness intensifies. A late dog walker, carrying a useful torch, thinks better of turning down towards the pond and sticks with the footpath that takes him towards the main road.

Talk in the public bar of The Three Casks turns to the strangers seen around the village of late. There is disagreement over who they might be.

"No idea what you're talking about, mate. Haven't seen anyone I didn't know."

"Come on, John. Every evening I see them, same clothes and whatever. Hanging around by the War Memorial or on the way to the pond."

"It'll be ramblers. Or that Nordic walking lark that Glenys does."

"I tell you, they look really odd."

"Well, I still don't know what you're on about."

Sophie dreads going into her bedroom. She does her homework at the kitchen table. She clings to her mother's arm when it's her bedtime. Inside her head, her voice screams, "Please help me. I don't know what to do. I'm so scared." But she mutely does as she has always done and kisses her parents, then walks up the stairs to her bedroom. Her feet are made of lead.

She follows her routine. Zipped tight inside her onesie, she pulls the duvet over her face and inhales the scent of fear. She mutters a few words of prayer to a God she doesn't know or understand. Then she waits, hoping that she will fall asleep before the landing lights go out.

She awakens to the sound of the church bell striking three o'clock. She keeps her body still, breathing silently, fighting the urge to peek out from under her covers. There is a dim light creeping into her room, a warm comforting kind of light. Then she notices her bed feels lighter. Normal. She moves her hand over the pillow and lifts her head a fraction. The bedroom door is open.

"Sophie. Sophie."

Someone is calling her. She squeezes her eyes shut tight but the light seems to penetrate inside her mind.

"Come with me, Sophie."

And her body is weightless, floating out of her bed, towards the ragged figure of a young woman who beckons her. A woman who smiles with crooked, blackened teeth. Whose hooked finger compels her to come closer until she is flying out of the window, out into the sky, the house is below her, they are speeding up, away towards the road and the trees are below her and she feels… nothing.

There are other ragged figures, other people dressed in all sorts of strange and ragged clothing, floating around, drifting aimlessly. Unseeing eyes flit back and forth, as if they are searching for something. The night-time scene is alive with spectres, some huddled in groups, others flying randomly about.

Then Sophie notices a pale glow in the distance. She feels the tug of welcome. The light brightens to blinding and she speeds towards it. It's all around her. And she hears the chatter of excited voices in her head.

"We've found it, we can go now. At last, we can go home. And Sophie can come with us."

There is a calm voice talking to her. It's a familiar voice although it doesn't seem to be her mother or her father or anyone she knows. The voice says, "Stay still and quiet. Pull the duvet back over your head and wait."

And beside her, unmistakeably, is the weight on the side of her bed again.

The church clock strikes four. An owl hoots outside her bedroom window. She is lying in bed. The weight settles and she notices it's like an anchor, securing her down to earth.

She wriggles further towards it and finds comfort in its heaviness. Her dream is still fresh in her mind but, for now, all is well.

"Have you had any trouble recently with your ghosts?"

"Now you mention it, I think we have. The house has been feeling distinctly unsettled of late. Like they are agitated and we've had a few mishaps like broken dishes and the toaster went kaput."

"I was talking to the vicar about it. His ghosts have been

moaning at him day and night. Complaining that the departed are not moving on as they should. He mentioned we might have to get those psychic people back, the ones who re-routed the ley line."

"What on earth are you talking about?"

"Oh, I thought it was common knowledge. The ley line that runs along Main Road gets stuck at Dusk Cottage and again at the church. The vicar says we need to get the energy flowing again so all these dead people who want to pass over can find their way to the nearest portal. It's like a meeting point for departed souls. It's over by the bend in Bromham Road. Where they used to hang up the highwaymen."

"You seem to know a lot about it."

"Only what the vicar told me. But I suppose most of the people who have lived here a long time know about it."

"And it's where they used to hang up the highwaymen?"

"Yes, I think it used to be called Gallows Corner."

"So why aren't the dead people going to this portal thingy?"

"Oh, didn't I explain? The ley line acts like a conduit helping departed souls to move swiftly towards their final destination. If it's blocked or weak, the souls lose their way. My ghosts have been up in arms about it, moaning and whinging. Say they can't get any peace and quiet with all these disoriented dead cluttering the place up."

"I suppose it's like having your unwanted relatives to stay and you can't get rid of them."

"Quite. So yours have been playing up? Everyone I speak to says the same thing. Lots of agitated ghosts."

"And what can be done about it, again?"

"Well, we get the psychic people back and they trace the energy for any obstructions or breakages. They use special copper wire to re-route around any blockages, like if somebody has built a new extension or dug up their drains or something. Then they get the energy whooshing along and everyone is happy again. The living and the dead and the ones who just prefer to hang around in our houses for the fun of it."

"I hope it works."

"It'll work fine, they know what they're doing. Parish Council will pay, of course."

"So that's what the extra bit of Council tax goes for."

"And the roads, Deidre, and the cricket pitch and mowing the verges and don't forget the village show."

"Quite."

Sophie lies on her bed in the sunshine with her hand gently smoothing the covers on the right hand side. As she smoothes, she can feel the weight move, hear the silky dress rustle, and a gentle touch makes her hand tingle. She has everything all worked out in her head. Her new friend has helped her to understand. The strange flying dream. The things she saw. The messages in her head. Now she knows. She doesn't have to tell anyone. But she's realised that most people already seem to know. It's the talk of the village.

The Wellingborough Witch
and the King of Croyland

N M Wogden

The two women stumbled from the Red Well pub and into the damp street, clutching one another for support. They'd watched the deluge from their seats by the window, in between glasses of wine, bites of food, talking and laughter.

The older of the two, Kelly, brushed her dirty blonde hairy from her face, grabbed her sister's hand and dragged her down the street.

"Where are we going, Kelly?" Vicki, her younger sister, groaned.

"Come on! I want to show you something! Come on!"

Vicki was very different to her sister. While her sister was tall and lanky, Vicki was quite short and not as thin, but the pair had always been close.

"Come on, Kelly! It's late! The rain may start again anytime soon."

But Kelly linked her arm and continued dragging her younger sister down the road.

"There's something I want to show you. You like all that horror stuff, don't you?"

Vicki rolled her eyes. Her fascination into the world beyond ours wasn't something her older sister truly understood. But Kelly continued to drag her down Silver Street, avoiding a car which had slowed right down as the two passed.

"Come on!" Vicki frowned. She just wanted to head home. Her sister was hammered and she wasn't much better. But Kelly was insistent she was going to show Vicki whatever it was.

"So there's a cool fact that, until forty-odd years ago, there was a zoo in Wellingborough."

And still Kelly pulled her down the street. "Recently, they put in some wooden animals to commemorate this and they put them in a park nearby."

Vicki groaned. The rain looked like it was going to start again any minute now, yet her sister was telling her boring stories about the town.

"They also put in some musical steps. Rumour has it, that a local witch... "

"What?" Vicki stopped walking and looked at her sister. "A witch?"

Kelly nodded.

"Like an actual, give you a poison apple, kind of witch?"

Kelly nodded and Vicki gave a snort of laughter. "A witch?" She laughed loudly, it echoing down the otherwise empty streets.

"It's true! Well, they say this witch cursed these animals so that if you were to play the right tune on the musical steps, the animals would come to life."

Kelly dragged her down a side road now, away from Sheep Street and the general direction of Vicki's flat.

"Are we off to see the witch then?"

Kelly laughed, stumbled and carried on.

"No, stupid. I'm off to show you the animals."

Vicki groaned and let her sister get ahead of her. She pulled her collar up against the wind, peering upwards at the sky, still expecting the rain to start again any minute.

"Come on!"

She saw Kelly disappear around a large building so frowned and jogged to catch up. As she did so, she peered up at the large building alongside her, feeling she was being watched.

Suddenly, from the darkness beyond, she could hear a beeping noise, mixed with Kelly's laughter.

She rounded the corner to see her sister not too far away, standing atop a set of six rubber stepping stones.

"Look!"

Kelly jumped high into the air and landed on one of the steps. As the step sunk down a musical note sounded.

"Haha! Good, isn't it?"

Vicki couldn't help but smile and chuckle as she watched Kelly jump from step to step, each time a different pitched note sounding out.

"Come on!"

Vicki sighed and looked around to see a small stone platform. She turned and saw that, because she was short, she was face to face with a large wooden lion. Ignoring the tune her sister was playing in the background, she looked closely at the lion in front of her. Slowly, she reached up and stroked his long snout, before smiling to herself and heading over to her sister.

"Look what I can play!"

Vicki wandered towards her sister, as she jumped, actually playing a tune that was half recognisable as something.

"Look what I can play!" Kelly shouted, jumping up and down, playing a half-recognisable tune.

"Whoa! That's good!"

Kelly nodded and spun in mid-air, before landing on another note and continuing to jump from step to step.

Vicki shook her head in amusement, then paused. She could hear heavy footfalls behind her. More than one set of heavy footfalls. She felt her heart almost stop.

It was dark. It was late. And they were alone.

Whatever it was began to growl behind her.

Feeling her heart in her throat, she turned.

A few feet away from her was a huge lion.

Made of wood. Taking each creaking step on its giant wooden paws.

Vicki realised, to her astonishment, that Kelly had been right. The musical steps had made the wooden lion come to life.

Vicki backed away, tripped over a tree root and fell sprawling across the ground. "No!" She must have drunk too much. She shut her eyes before opening them again, hoping it would be gone.

But the giant wooden lion continued to advance on her, its long wooden fangs now bared in a snarl.

"Kelly!" she screamed.

Vicki was still lying flat on her back.

Kelly tried to run, but she couldn't –

She was rooted to the spot, staring at the lion. She could

only watch as it clamped its jaws around her sister's throat, blood shooting out across the grass.

Screams echoed across the empty park. Then, suddenly, they didn't.

Unable to move, Kelly watched as the lion pushed Vicki's body aside with his large head and, very slowly, turned its large wooden head towards her.

Then something over the lion's wooden head caught her eye.

Standing on the path, was an old woman, wearing a black wooden cloak, holding a wooden staff.

At last, she found her voice. "Help me!"

The lion advanced. The old woman, very slowly, shook her head, raised her staff and banged it loudly on the ground.

Immediately, the wooden lion pounced on Kelly, who fell to the ground, screaming. The lion began to feast on her.

And so the Wellingborough Witch claimed two victims for her own.

The Wellingborough Witch and the Mysterious Monks

N M Wogden

The bells of All Hallows Church chimed eight o'clock loudly nearby but, inside the office, Barry Turnball turned over another piece of paper on the memo he was meant to be reading, having not really taken in a single word.

He sighed deeply, leaned back in his chair, pulled off his glasses and ran his fingers down his face, groaning.

Why was he still at work? His colleagues had gone home hours ago. Heck, even the cleaners were finishing now. He could hear them over the hammering of the rain outside, shouting their farewells. Yet here he was, still working.

This was probably why his wife had left him for another man. He didn't blame her, really, he'd always been one for long hours to get the job done.

Barry sighed, falling forwards on his chair and putting his glasses back on. He looked out of the window and saw, not the rain lashing down, but his own reflection. He looked haggard, worn down, his hair was thinning on top and his eyes nearly always had bags under them these days. He looked around the small office he shared with four others. He was completely alone. He closed his eyes, deciding, perhaps, he should call it a night.

Then he heard the floorboard down the corridor creak loudly, causing him to freeze, stock still, where he sat.

Maybe he was not alone, after all.

Frowning, Barry stared through the glass in the door that led to the corridor outside.

He'd just heard the cleaners leave. In fact, Martha had even popped in to say they were done for the night.

Then the floorboard creaked again.

He got to his feet, crept to the door, pulled it open as fast as he could.

As the light in the hall was turned off, Barry squinted, trying to make out if anyone was there. He paused, looking up and down the corridor. Then he heard another creak down the hall. Barry ran his hand along the wall, searching for the light switch. He turned it on, but the lightbulb blew, making him jump.

He could hear a noise.

As the noise grew, Barry frowned and shook his head.

Somewhere in the building, he could hear Gregorian chants. But that was impossible. There hadn't been any monks in this building for decades.

Slowly, he made his way down the corridor, sweat trickling down his back.

Then, across the light of the emergency exit, a hooded figure walked past and the solo chanting of one monk grew even louder.

Barry broke into a run, reached the end of the corridor and skidded around it.

The hooded figure was at the other end of the corridor, still striding away, his thick woollen robe dragging along the carpeted floor.

"Hello?" Barry heard his voice break as he spoke. He

tried to swallow but his throat was very dry. "Hello? Who's there?"

But his voice echoed down the stone corridors and there was no reply. Instead, the chanting was fading away.

Barry paused. He was losing it. He'd been working too much and now his overtiredness was causing him to hallucinate. He pulled off his glasses, leant against the wall, wiped them on his shirt.

It was time for him to leave. He would go home, have a microwave meal, feed the cat, watch some comedy programme online.

He made his way back to his office and turned the door handle.

He turned the handle again. But it didn't budge. Frowning, he put his shoulder behind it and pushed.

But still the door would not move.

Now, he was scared. The door didn't even have a lock and yet it had locked itself.

Barry fumbled in his pocket, then realised he'd left his phone in his office.

Deciding he now just needed to get out of here, he ran back down the corridor.

The chanting had started again and, this time, it was clear it was more than one monk. It echoed from all down the corridor. He was surrounded.

He clasped his hands over his ears and yelled, "STOP IT! STOP IT! STOP IT! STOP IT!"

He looked down the corridor again, thinking about making a break for the fire exit. Then he saw them.

Standing in front of the fire exit were two monks.

Both wearing long brown robes, with their hoods pulled right the way over, both repeating the Gregorian chanting again and again.

Slowly, step by step, they made their way down the corridor towards him.

"NO!"

Barry was on his feet, running for his life, away from them, as fast as his legs could take him. He slammed hard into the wall and ran down the corridor.

He reached some stairs, nearly falling as he ran down them, the sound of monks chanting getting louder and louder in his ears.

All he knew was that the main entrance had glass on the front door. If he could smash that, he could escape.

However, when he burst into the main atrium, he stopped dead in his tracks, the blood draining from his face.

There were twenty – no, thirty – monks in here, all of them chanting their Gregorian chant.

He spun back round, intent on finding a cupboard to hide in, when he saw the two monks were only feet behind him.

But Barry could see the door and, slowly, began to step towards it.

He was thinking he might make it when, just as they were at their loudest and closing in, they stopped. An eerie silence filled the hall.

Then, every single monk turned to face him.

Barry was rooted to the spot. The hooded monks didn't move. All of them just watched him.

Barry looked up at the door.

She was hunched, wearing a long black cloak, holding a crooked wooden staff. She had a long nose, blood shot red eyes and very little hair.

Slowly, she raised a long, gnarly looking finger and pointed directly at Barry.

From under their cloaks, the monks pulled out long wooden planks of wood, long pieces of rope and long wooden brooms. The old woman raised her wooden staff and banged once loudly on the ground.

"NO!"

As the monks circled him, they began their chanting again. He spun wildly, but everywhere he tried he could see only the monks.

He was hit in the back by a piece of rope. He screamed. He was smashed in the stomach by handle of the old woman's broom. He was whipped, smashed, poked, punched and stabbed from he didn't know where.

He crumpled to the floor. But they did not stop. They attacked him again and again and again – until Barry felt no more.

And so, the Wellingborough Witch claimed another victim.

The Wellingborough Witch and the Crone in the Chair

N M Wogden

Maude Clementine sat quite happily by her living room window, drinking her last cup of Earl Grey before turning in for the night.

The sky outside was blood red. She sat enjoying the colours, three floors up in her small home in Croyland Flats.

She lived alone, her husband, Albert, having died of a heart attack suddenly ten years ago.

She took another long sip of her tea and noticed she'd put in a bit too much sugar for her liking. She glanced down at the newspaper on her lap and the pictures of the two young women and the middle-aged man stared back at her, as they had every day over the past few weeks.

This troubled her. The whole article troubled her. She'd read it several times, of course. The whole town had.

Three murders in less than a week in Wellingborough was completely unheard of, even to Maude. Her family had lived in Wellingborough for generations, nearly always going to the same local schools as well. There was something about this town that pulled her family back to it eventually – even the ones who'd tried to escape it.

As she looked down at the paper, she went over the troubling thought again.

She'd been here, the night those two girls were torn to

121

bits by wild animals. Surely, they must have screamed out? Why hadn't she heard them?

And the man. Beaten to death by several blunt instruments only a few buildings away. Surely someone must have heard something, even if it wasn't her.

Yet Maude knew nothing of what had transpired in those evenings. It was a complete blank. In fact, it was as if she had blacked out completely. She couldn't remember anything about the days in question at all.

As Maude stirred her tea around in the cup, thoughts of those people being attacked swirled around her head.

Maude knew all the local stories of course – witches, ghosts, undead animals, all of which her mother had told her when she was a young child. But they came back to her now, in her mother's sternest voice. "These stories have got to come from somewhere, Maude."

But the old woman shook her head. It was absurd. She could barely get to the kitchen any more, let alone summon dead creatures. Chuckling, she had another sip of tea, before frowning, realising she'd let it go cold.

Maude gave the evening up and decided, as it was just past nine, it was time she got ready for bed. She pushed herself to her feet and had just put on her carpet slippers, when she heard a knock at the door.

Sighing, she shuffled across to her Zimmer frame and towards the door as fast as she could, which was to say, not that fast at all. Whoever it was, knocked three times more before she could reach it.

Unbolting the door, she slid it open a few inches. "Yes?"

Two young police officers stood there, an older female

officer and a younger Asian man. The woman officer smiled broadly. "Oh, hello there."

Maude gave a small smile. "Hello, my dear. How may I help you?"

The woman said, very slowly, "My name is Sergeant Melanie Maguire. This is Police Constable Wrong." The male officer scowled at his colleague. "Would it be okay if you could answer some questions for us, please?"

Frightened, Maude nodded. Did they know about the black-outs?

"Thank you. You don't happen to remember what happened on the evening of the 24th and 31st of March?"

"I'm sorry, my dear," she lied. "I don't even remember what I had for breakfast anymore."

The woman smiled. "That's all right, my dear." The woman smiled, then shouted, carefully enunciating every syllable, "That's all right, my dear. I'll just slip you my card." She handed it over. "If you remember anything, just give us a ring and someone can pop over to talk to you."

Maude smiled again and raised the card. "Thank you. I will."

"Lovely. Have a pleasant evening." The two officers turned away and, as Maude was closing the door, she heard the male officer say, "All right, so no dead body. But give it a few weeks and maybe there will be."

Maude scowled at him and shut the door. She hobbled away again, but as she got to her small bathroom, she heard another knock on the door.

However, it did not sound like a person knocking, but rather someone banging with something hard.

Maude hobbled to the door. But whoever it was, did not knock again. She opened it to find the hallway completely deserted. No sign of anyone.

Maude sighed and shut the door. Again, she began back down the hallway, when she heard a noise coming from her living room, like nails on a chalk board.

Maude felt her fragile heart increase its beat as she hobbled towards the room. It was dark now, so she turned on one of the lamps, which quickly went out again.

"Maude... "

A low sinister voice echoed throughout the flat and Maude stopped still in her tracks.

She'd forgotten to close the curtains in the living room and, carved into the glass of the window, were four words.

"It is time again."

Maude was terrified, then remembered the card in her hand. She was only a few feet from her chair, which was next to her phone, so she hobbled towards it and picked it up

She got a constant tone, which told her the line was dead. She glanced up, suddenly remembering the emergency cord in her bathroom. But before she could get to her feet, the voice echoed through the flat, as though it were coming from inside the walls.

"Maude."

Maude was rooted to her chair. Slow footsteps in her hallway, closely followed by the clunk of wood on wood.

"I must feast again."

The voice spoke out, but now not from the walls of the flat, but from the hall way. Its pitch had also risen an octave, to the level of an owl's screech.

The voice who spoke was higher pitched than her own.

"It is time."

Clunk! Clunk! – sounded from the hall again.

Maude couldn't move. Not even if she wanted to. It was as if someone had frozen her completely. She watched, in horror as the door of her living-room creaked open.

Standing there, was a black, cloaked, hooded figure, holding a wooden staff.

Clunk! Clunk! With each step, the hooded figure came in the room.

Breathing hard, Maude eventually managed to speak.

"Who... Who... Who are you?"

Clunk! Clunk! The figure stepped nearer.

"I am," the female voice said – like her own voice but even more highly pitched than before – "the Wellingborough Witch. It is time again. I hunger."

Maude stared up. The woman reached a thin, liver spotted old hand up and slowly threw back her hood.

As Maude stared up into the face she knew all too well, her scream was lost in her throat.

"We hunger."

In a horribly twisted smile, Maude's own face stared back at her.

With her long, gnarled staff, the Witch thumped twice on the floor.

Maude vanished.

The Witch smiled, cackled, banged her staff three times.

And now the Wellingborough Witch was ready to claim another.

The Ghost Writer

Gordon Adams

I had been asked to come to his home, set deep within the Northamptonshire countryside. I needed to talk him face-to-face, at length. My task as a ghost writer was to engage him in conversation, to find out as much as I could about his life so I could write his life story. But when he swivelled round in his chair to face me, I realised I already knew it.

"Ah, you're here at last, my friend! I seem to have been waiting forever for you."

In the half-light, he reached out his wrinkled hand. He clearly wanted to shake mine, but I froze. I couldn't take my eyes off his face. Even in the half-light, I recognised that face instantly. He looked very old and tired now, but this was a face I couldn't help but recognise.

It was my own face.

"Why do you look so surprised, my friend? Who else would I send for? Who can better report my story than myself?"

His grey eyes latched on to mine.

"No-one can do a better evaluation of you than I. After all, who understands you better than me?"

I couldn't move. I feel sure my heart stopped that very moment, the moment I first realised I was dead.

At the back of my mind was a distant, hazy memory. I

remembered going to bed last night and feeling a sudden pain in my chest. The rest was a blur. I knew, though, that this was no dream. This was real.

"What... what are you?" I stammered.

"There's no need to be afraid, my friend. Really! I am exactly who I seem to be. I am you and you are me. Just as we were, at different points in our existence. You know, I've spent half of eternity waiting for you to arrive this time – at least it seems like it. Things do get terribly dull, you know, when the blood stops pumping!

"Now I'd like to hear about your life. My life. Only... well, your recollection of it. Let's start with the juicy bits, shall we? The most interesting moments. We've so much to review, haven't we? So many unpleasant actions, really. So much bitterness. All that wanton destruction of other people's lives. You really have gone to town!"

* * * * *

Now I understood that cryptic remark from my agent. I'd asked about the subject of this latest autobiography.

"Oh, you'll know him the instant you get there!"

It was nothing new, this kind of cloak and dagger stuff, when a celebrity was involved. Often they didn't want their friends to know what they were doing until the autobiography had been finished to their complete satisfaction. They wanted to have their own version of events to show the world. They certainly didn't want any ex-partners or lovers getting in on the act. They wanted to control exactly what was written, hoping to come across as a half-decent human being. Despite the facts.

So I wasn't surprised to be sent to meet this man with only the briefest of briefings. Nor was I surprised his name was withheld from me in advance. But nothing could have prepared me for the shock of meeting a much older version (or so it seemed) of myself.

Many hours passed, with the two of us speaking in the half-light.

He wanted to hear everything from my perspective. He was particularly interested in every act of unpleasantness, every hurtful remark, every unkind action I had ever made. The entire time we conversed, his eyes were locked on mine. I felt like he was staring into my soul.

As time passed, I realised I was going to have to write this all up in elaborate detail. It dawned on me that this book was going to take a very, very long time to write.

He was asking the questions, not me. But he added to my answers.

A row with my wife: "That hurt you a lot, didn't it? Who else did it hurt?"

Or whenever my answer was circumspect: "I think you may have omitted someone from this story. Have you perhaps forgotten to mention someone else – someone who was really rather important?"

He asked me to relive the bitterness of my divorce: the hurt meted out to my children; to recall again the anger directed towards my ex-wife and her young lover. He asked me to talk through every detail of the fight we two men had, that night we came together outside the Hind Hotel, spilling blood on to the streets of Wellingborough. He prompted me to relive all the punches and the kicks, to recall the anguish of my children watching on and screaming the night their Daddy kicked lumps out of Mummy's new boyfriend.

I'd enjoyed it at the time, but I didn't enjoy retelling that story. The Boy Wonder had simply got what was coming to him, hadn't he? And he had recovered soon enough: he was only off work for a couple of weeks. Perhaps I should have kicked him harder?

"How long did it take your children to recover?" asked the old man.

I'd never thought of that before.

And on we went.

* * * * *

After our conversation was over, the old man pointed to a desk in the corner of the room. He held up a golden fountain pen and indicated a large pile of white paper by the side of the desk.

"Now, it's time to do what you do best!" he said. "I know what a good writer you are. Try to make your readers engage with this character, for all his flaws. He has done so many terrible things, but he has been human, after all. And perhaps, somewhere deep inside, he has a conscience?"

I think I saw a tear form in the old man's eye.

"Try to make your readers empathise with this character. That is going to be important, if you only knew who was going to read this book. So very, very important."

* * * * *

I don't know how many days I spent writing. I worked non-stop, without a break. For some reason, I didn't seem to get hungry or tired. Finally, a small mountain of papers was piled up high in front of me, all covered with my handwriting.

My task was finally over. I placed my pen down with a weary sigh. "It is done."

"Then sign your name here," said the old man excitedly. "This is your life story – *our* life story – after all. It should bear the author's name, shouldn't it? Despite it being *ghost-written*!"

He laughed long and hard at his own joke.

I signed the bottom of the document.

"Now, I will have the pleasure of being the first to read it," said the old man. He leaned slowly back in his armchair and flipped to the first page.

"I will need to read this very carefully and reflect. I must decide if this person has learned from his life's experiences, you see? Much depends on this."

I had an important question, but didn't dare ask it. Instead, I asked another, simpler question. "What do you want me to do while you are reading?"

"Oh, you have plenty more writing still to do, my friend."

I stared at him.

"I want you to write this story again – now – from the perspective of the other characters. Each and every one of them."

131

He smiled, his yellow teeth flashing at me.

"Take your time. There's no hurry. *You have all the time in the world!*"

A Winning Lottery Ticket

Jason McClean

A winning lottery ticket.

Terry was a winner.

Not the main lottery on a Saturday, or even a Friday night. This was the scratchcard lottery. A ticket that cost £5 and promised one in every 3.58 people would win a prize of some description.

Terry was one of the 3.58 people.

He bought a lottery ticket every Friday on the way home from his work as a shop assistant in *HMV* in Kettering. It was a treat, along with the sausage and chips from the Texas Grill next door.

It was always the same bingo scratchcard game he played. He'd won a tenner the first time and then after a barren spell, another £30. It paid out. It was his lucky game.

You had to match the numbers like a game of bingo. The prizes built up like bingo too. Get a line and it was a tenner. Get two lines and it was £30. Get a diagonal and it was £50 and the four corners payed out a cool £10,000.

He scratched diligently while Cara and George fought amongst themselves. Loud, but totally silent to Terry, switched off in his own world.

The end of a hard week, the scratchcard lottery, the five minutes of hope he allowed himself, he savoured. He let the distractions of everyday life flow around him. Just for five minutes.

He got two lines quickly, then two rows followed. Three corners fell into place then another row and column, a diagonal falling into place too.

He needed a 75 to hit the last corner. To give him four corners, or better than that, a full house. The 20 pence in his fingers cleared the last number and there it was, proud as Punch. A 75.

A full house.

£1 million pounds, tax free.

Options.

Hopes.

Dreams.

Freedom.

He quickly checked all the numbers again. And then again. He had a full house. A winning lottery ticket.

He checked the rules of the game while Cara bounced around the kitchen laughing and George tittered with glee.

A full house wins £1 million pounds. Please redeem at your local National Lottery outlet or call this number. Please have your scratchcard at the ready when calling as you will be asked to verify the win.

Terry grabbed his mobile phone, never far away. He couldn't punch in the numbers, his hands were shaking that hard.

"What's up, Tel?" asked Sarah, his wife, drying towel and dish in hand.

"Here, take the phone, dial these numbers."

Sarah carefully placed the dish down, keeping a grip on

the towel, and took the phone from Terry's quivering hand.

She pressed the numbers he called and handed it back.

Cara and George were silent, staring at their parents. There was a current of electricity in the room. They could feel it. Something was happening. Maybe important. Enough to stop playing and take notice.

"Hello, can I speak with Camelot, please?" said Terry.

"Yes."

A muffled voice on the phone.

"Yes, I think so," said Terry.

"OK," he confirmed.

"Yes, there's a number on the back."

Terry read it out slowly into the phone. And then again when he was asked to confirm it.

Sarah, George and Cara remained silent, watching. Plugged into the live wire of tension and excitement.

"OK, so I should wait here?"

"OK, see you soon."

Terry put the phone down and it skittered on the table, his hands shaking furiously.

"What is it?" demanded Sarah, picking up a coffee mug and drying it on autopilot.

"They said I'm not allowed to tell anyone. Not until they get here."

"Terry. I. Am. Your. Wife."

"I know, but they said to tell no-one."

"Terry."

"OK, don't tell anyone else."

"Tell them what?"

"I have won a million quid. On a scratchcard."

The room amped up to ten and three pairs of eyes bulged.

"Are you sure?"

"No. I won't believe it until they get here. Until they actually transfer the money into my bank account. It would be just my luck that it's wrong or something."

"But, Dad," said Cara. "You had to tell them a code. That means they have already checked – did they say you had won?"

"Yes, they did," said Terry. "But I don't believe it. Not yet. I need the money in my bank first."

Cara hugged George tight. George was smiling like a hyena, eyes betraying a million possibilities the money could bring.

"How long before they get here?" asked Cara. At sixteen years old, she had a proper grasp on what difference a million pounds could make to her life. Clothes, the latest mobile phone, bags galore and a decent car when she passed her test. The opportunities were endless.

George was two years younger but, if anything, his horizons were expanding even faster than his sister. Widescreen TV, the latest games console with every game he wanted, the latest mobile phone, a new bike and a pair of the most expensive trainers he could find. Perfect.

"The nearest agent is in Burton Latimer, he should be here shortly."

"Just a minute," said Sarah, no hint of a smile. "You said *your* bank account."

Smiles vanished off the children's faces instantly but reappeared almost immediately.

"You'll still share it with us, won't you, Dad?" said Cara.

There was a pause before Terry said, "Don't worry, you'll get a treat if I get the money. What do you want? A new phone maybe?"

"And the rest, Dad," exclaimed Cara. "There is an incredible bag from Jimmy Choo that would smack the other girls down at school. And what about a holiday somewhere – New York for a shopping trip? The whole family?"

"I need the latest phone too, Dad," burst in George. "I'd be the only one at school with one, booyah."

Sarah placed the coffee mug down and picked up another one that needed drying, hands rubbing carefully, muscle memory, she wasn't even aware she was doing it. "And what about me?" she asked, steel in her voice.

Terry smiled coolly at her. "What would you like? A weekend spa with you mum? How about a new car? That old Ford is starting to cost more than it is worth. We could find you a nice new one, only a couple of years old."

"What about my car, Dad?" asked Cara. "I'll be taking my test soon. I don't want an old banger. I want something neat. How about a brand new Mini?"

"Hold on a minute!" exclaimed Terry, hands held up in surrender. "Stop spending all my money before I even have it. It may all come to nothing yet. They need to verify the scratchcard."

The doorbell chimed.

"That can't be them already," said Terry, sweating, gripping the scratchcard.

"I'll see," said George, bounding out of the room.

137

Cara stood stock still, Terry sat and sweated, Sarah was now drying a lunch box lid.

"No, it's *only* Grandma," shouted George from the front door.

Shuffling sounds came from the hallway into the tense silence of the kitchen. A sloppy sounding slurp as Grandma kissed George and the rustle of a hasty sleeve wiping it away.

"What's going on here?" demanded Grandma, bent nearly double, stooping as she walked in the kitchen. "Someone been killed? Or married?"

Grandma laughed at her own joke.

Silence.

"What's that you've got in your hand there, Dinger?" Grandma always liked to prod her son-in-law by calling him Dinger – as Terry, Tel, telephone, ringer and eventually Dinger. She had an instinctive knack of knowing what irritated and then would tease it with pleasure.

"Nothing for you to worry about," bristled Terry.

"It's a winning lottery scratch card, Mum," said Sarah. "A million quid by the looks of it, we've hit it big."

"Have we indeed," said Grandma. "Money can't buy you happiness, Dinger. You might wish you'd never got that ticket. Would you like me to look after it for you?"

"Thanks, but no thanks." Terry gave her a winning smile.

"Tell Grandma what we are going to buy with the money," suggested George.

Terry gave the boy a hard stare. "I'm buying nothing with the money. I've agreed to nothing."

"But we are a family," said Sarah, pulling a plate from

138

the pile and rubbing it gently with the dish cloth. "We should all decide what is best to spend it on. I'm sure we could splash out on a new sofa for you, Mum. You've been after one for ages."

Terry snorted.

"What was that for?" demanded Sarah, clanging the plate down with a little too much force. Everyone looked at her. The electricity was turning dark, nasty.

"Don't worry about me," said Grandma. "I'd settle for a cup of tea."

"I'll get you one, Grandma," said Cara, making her way to the kettle.

"Here, use this." Sarah handed her daughter a freshly dried mug.

"Yes, make Granny a nice cup of tea," said Terry. Grandma did not like being called Granny. She hated it. Terry knew that.

"So what are you going to spend it on then, Dinger?" asked Grandma. "You've been promising Sarah a full house decoration for years. Or is it going to be a new house now you have the cash?"

"I've better things than that to spend the money on," snapped Terry.

Silence.

The doorbell rang.

"That might be Camelot," exclaimed Terry.

"I'll get it." George bounded out of the room.

The door opened.

Hushed voices.

"Dad, it's a man from Camelot. He says he wants to see

you."

Terry shot up and left the room, grasping his scratchcard.

A minute passed and George came back in, followed by a middle-aged man in a grey suit. He was clearly happy in his job, a huge smile painted on his face.

"Well done, folks," he said. "My name is Jim. I work for Camelot and I'm here to verify the scratchcard. I wouldn't half like a cup of tea if there's one going?"

"Make Jim a cup of tea," instructed Terry, pulling a chair out for the guest.

Cara bristled at the command but Sarah quickly dried another mug and passed it across.

"You know what I love about my job," carried on Jim, oblivious to the tension. "I meet winners every day of the week. People whose lives are changed dramatically by the money they win. If you have a winning ticket, then things are really going to change for you all. We haven't had many jackpots in Kettering or Corby, so it would make my day for this ticket to be a winner."

"Can you check the ticket please," said Terry, placing it in front of Jim. "The suspense is killing me."

"Of course." Jim took a mobile phone out of his jacket pocket, just as the mug of tea arrived. "Thank you, little lady."

Grandma slurped her tea as Jim scanned the barcode on the scratchcard.

"No signal here," said Jim. "Do you have a wifi code I could use? I need to send the scan through to our central computer. It then sends me a message, which is either a yes or a no. Right now I can't get any signal."

"I'll get the code," said George, bounding out to the router in the hallway and then bounding back in again with a little card emblazoned with the code. "I sure hope it says yes. I really want a new phone, same as the one you have."

"Thanks," said Jim, taking the wifi code. "Let me get that sorted now... Yes, it's a great phone and you'll be able to afford a lot of them if you have won the jackpot."

Terry snorted.

Cara shook her head.

Grandma slurped angrily.

Sarah picked up a sparkling clean pot and started drying.

"That did the trick. I'm connecting now."

Grandma slurped her tea again and Terry stared daggers at her.

"Now, folks, when it comes to winners, there are some really important things that you need to consider," said Jim. "Assuming the card is a winner, you will need to think about which bank account you want the money paid into. It has to be the person who purchased the card. And we always ask if that person would like their name in the paper with a picture."

"Sounds good to me," growled Terry.

"Ah, but sometimes it's not so good, so you need to take a bit of time to think it over," explained Jim. "Winners can quickly become losers if everyone they know starts asking for handouts or a few pounds here or there to help with some medical treatment or to pay the rent. If you let everyone know you're a winner, there can be downsides as well as ups. You'll certainly find out who your friends are – and you are likely to have a lot more friends than you ever thought possible. Money has a way of helping you make friends."

Jim's phone made a ping noise, like a text had been received. He placed down his cup of tea and looked intently at the screen.

"Another thing you need to consider is wealth management," he continued. "We can put you in touch with advisors who will assist you in how to invest the money and make the most of it."

Jim smiled a twinkle in his eye. "And that is exactly what we will have to do because the scratchcard is a winner. Well done. You are now millionaires."

Sarah dropped her pot and cloth and hugged Grandma. Cara and George whooped and hugged.

Terry smiled, deep and disturbing, eyes flitting left and right, as if looking for a route to escape.

"I do love my job," said Jim. "So what I'll do is leave this winner's form here for you to sign. It guides you through everything you need to know about winning, including tips and advice on accounts, media, whether you should keep on working or retire, that sort of thing. I urge you to read it, because the immediate feeling may be to give up the job and go on a cruise. But most winners don't do that. They like the social aspect of work and the daily routine. Are you ready to change all of that?"

"Yes, I am," said Terry, taking the sheet and scratchcard. "When do I hand this in? When do I get the money?"

Jim stood up, draining the last of his tea. "Thank you for that cuppa, young miss," he said, nodding to Cara. "It was just what I needed." He turned to Terry and Sarah. "Now, I want you to read that document and if I come by at, say, noon, tomorrow, we can go through it together and make sure everything is answered and correct.

"Read the bits about the children carefully. Coming in to a lot of money can destabilise them if not handled correctly. There are some tough decisions to make. It'll take about an hour to go through everything and then I'll authorise the bank transfer which should land in your account first thing on Monday morning and leave you lucky winners to start enjoying the rest of your lives. Well done again, folks."

"Not much well done if you ask me," stabbed Grandma. "A lucky ticket is all we got, nothing earned here, just pure luck."

"Absolutely, Madam," said Jim. "But well done, nonetheless."

George escorted Jim to the front door.

Grandma slurped the dregs of her tea. Noisily.

Cara looked between her mum and dad and said nothing.

Sarah grabbed a saucepan and wiped the suds off it.

Terry grasped the paper and the scratchcard close to his chest and sat down. "I'll take a coffee now," he said.

"You can get it yourself," screeched Grandma. "What sort of example is that to set the children, not so much as a please in sight. Money hasn't made you a better person, has it?"

"Leave him alone, Mum," pleaded Sarah. "Now's a time to be happy, not argue. We have a lot to think about before Jim comes back tomorrow. I don't even know if I'm going back to work on Monday. I'll certainly be buying a dishwasher as soon as the money clears. I've had enough years of washing up."

"A dishwasher is not something I'll be buying," harrumphed Terry. "I'll not be wasting money on things we don't need. I'll not be wasting a penny of it."

Sarah picked up a handful of spoons and started drying them, looking out the window, taking a deep breath.

"I'll be honest, Sarah, it's not like we've been happy for the last few months, maybe even a year," said Terry.

"Maybe this is what you need to find that happiness again," suggested Grandma softly. "Maybe the cash will get rid of the pressure."

"I don't think so," said Terry. "And while I am being honest, I had best say you don't help things one bit. Now I've got a bit of money, you want a piece of me. Five minutes ago, you were staring down your nose at me like a bit of dirt. I think you are a lot to do with why we are unhappy. Sarah doesn't do a thing without consulting you. Sometimes I think I'm married to you and that isn't a nice prospect."

The air in the room crackled. Grandma's mouth was open. It normally was open, but this time it was slack too.

Sarah put down the spoons and picked up a pile of forks that needed drying, losing herself in routine.

"So I think what I'll do is fill in this form myself," said Terry standing up. He pointed at George. "You are nothing more than a spoilt brat who runs to his mother any time he wants anything – and she caves in all the time. You know why I never used to have any money? Because of you. Forget the phone, kid. You'll not see a penny of this cash unless you earn it and that's the best lesson a father can give his son. Especially you."

The he turned to Cara. "As for you and your list of demands as long as your arm. What have you done to deserve any of them? You're nothing more than the image of your mother and granny and when I say that, I'm not paying you a compliment. It's about time you grew up and took responsibility for yourself.

"As for getting you a car to terrorise other drivers, you can forget that. Get a job and buy your own second-hand clunker and make the sacrifices to afford the insurance, the way I had to when I was your age. It's all part of learning. Don't think me winning money will bail you out. Life's already too easy for you. Why should you have everything handed to you?"

Spittle flecked from Terry's mouth, his face contorted.

George was trying to be brave.

Cara was sobbing softly, eyes like saucers.

Grandma still had an open mouth.

Sarah picked up the last plate and wiped it.

"As soon as I get my winnings, I'm out of here. I'm not going to be dragged down by the lot of you. Held me back for years you have. I should never have had kids, never wanted them, but you talked me into it, Sarah. I should never have married you in the first place. That was my biggest mistake ever."

George bolted from the room, Cara following him at a run, slamming the door behind her. Footsteps pounded up the stairs and doors banged.

"Look what you've done to the young ones," shrieked Grandma. "You can't mean that. What's got into you?"

"Shut up, old woman," sneered Terry. "If I never see them again, it'll be too soon, but mark my words, they'll be calling me all the time for money. They can sing all they like, they'll get nothing and neither will you."

Terry turned to Sarah. "As soon as I get my money, I'll get my solicitor to contact you. I'll be taking my half of the house with me. You had better get saving and do less shopping. You're going to need the money if you want to pay the mortgage by yourself."

Terry paused, looked at the two stricken women and said, "I feel great getting that lot off my chest, been building up. I'm a winner and will not be dragged down by you losers. I'll be off to The Peacock now, I think I deserve a pint to celebrate."

He eyed both women and added, "Don't bother waiting up. As Jim says, money helps you make new friends. I have a feeling I'll make a new friend tonight."

Grandma shook her head.

Sarah, tears running down her face, dropped the drying towel and revealed a sparkling paring knife, the last of the washing up. Designed to slice through meat, it had a four-inch blade that was razor sharp.

She took the single step towards her husband and buried the blade fully into his left eye socket.

Terry stood stock still, as if in disbelief, maybe for a whole second, before his other eye turned up in his head and he fell to the ground, straight down, no thrashing, no sound, just instantly dead. Blood pumped from the eye socket and created a small puddle on the tiled floor. The flood gradually slowed and then stopped.

A moment passed.

"Pick that up," said Grandma, pointing at the scratchcard and paperwork. "Quickly, you don't want blood on it."

Sarah obeyed and picked up the paperwork. She placed it on the table. Sounds of crying came from upstairs.

"Now be quick," said Grandma. "Get him out of the kitchen and into the garage. Try to keep his head off the floor, it'll make a mess. I'll get in here cleaned up before the kids come back down."

"I've killed him, Mum."

"And not a moment too soon either, my love. He had it coming. How could he say that to you all? He was evil."

"But I've killed him. I didn't mean to."

"No, and that's because you're a good person, but now you have to think about George and Cara. If they see this, it's game over for all of you. You can't let that happen. Now get the body into the garage while I clean up. We'll deal with everything else later."

Sarah nodded and walked over to the internal door that led to the utility room, which in turn led to the garage. With tears flowing and considerable effort, she pulled the body into the garage and threw an old blanket over it.

She wasn't crying for Terry. He didn't deserve her tears. She was crying for herself. For what she had done. For what she had become. A killer.

Grandma had a mop in full swing. Sarah grabbed kitchen roll and got busy.

It took less than five minutes to clean the floor, sparkling, smelling of lemons. The sound of crying upstairs continued. Both kids were together in a single room, probably holding each other. Righteous anger flushed Sarah's guilt away.

Grandma opened the kitchen door, walked down the hallway faster than her years would have suggested, then opened the front door on to Nelson Street, before slamming it shut. She came back to the kitchen.

"That was Terry leaving. That's what you tell everyone now. The children, Terry's work when they call on Monday, Jim when he comes back tomorrow. Terry has left and is never coming back."

Sarah nodded.

"Now, call the kids, let them know he's left for good. Tell them he had a change of heart and left the winning scratchcard, but wants a new life and they aren't to look for him."

"They won't believe it."

"They will when he never shows up again. He left the house and will never be coming back."

"Okay."

"And dry your eyes."

"Okay."

Sarah and Grandma hugged.

"You're not a loser," said Grandma. "You're a winner."

Grandma pressed the winning scratchcard into Sarah's hand.

"Right now... You've just won big."

Sarah thought of Terry and the pain he had inflicted on his children. Her children. On her. She smiled.

She was a winner.

She opened the door and called Cara and George to come down, their dad was gone.

The four of them. Winners or losers? In it together.

And a winning lottery ticket.

The Afterparty

James Dart

The thump on my bumper snapped me out of my alcohol-induced fit of giggling. I was pretty far gone by that point. I had been to a party in Roade and, five pints of Special Brew and a few shots of vodka later, was driving back towards Blisworth through that country road with no bloody lights.

I was fine to drive. I really was. It was three in the morning, nobody else was on the road and it wasn't like I lived far away. It should have been fine.

But he had to step out into the road in the dark, even wearing dark clothes, if you can believe it. My lights were on, so he couldn't claim lack of vision as an excuse. Yes, sir, he was one dumb arsehole…

One dumb dead arsehole…

My mind is a pretty sharp one so, even while bladdered, I had the wherewithal to pull over and check on the stupid prat. I even knew what to do; I shone the torch on my phone in his face. Wasn't breathing, from what I could see, and his eyelids were closed very loosely, like doors left slightly ajar.

It was my opinion he was, as I think is the technical term, screwed.

So here I am, crouching at the side of the road like a bear in the woods, staring down at a cadaver. I could go to prison for this. The law of this country is stupid and lacking in common sense. I was well over the drink-driving limit, an excuse for police to push people who haven't done anything wrong around, if you ask me, and, despite the fact this is entirely the dead dipshit's fault, I would be done for death by dangerous driving.

Of course, that's if they knew it was me. There were no witnesses, the speed cameras didn't even work. The only ones who know what happened here tonight are the two us, very soon to become the one of us, if it hadn't already. There are some bushes at the side of the road. He probably wouldn't be found for days. The stupid sod would probably thank me; he might appear on one of those unsolved mystery shows on telly, have Derrick O' what-his-name try to speak to him from beyond the grave.

Heh, yeah… poor sap would be more notable in death than he ever was in life.

So, I give him a kick (no fingerprints here, coppers) into the bushes, cover him up and stroll back to my car. Walking is something of a challenge, but, like I said, I have a sharp mind. Getting back into the car, my sharp mind turns to driving mode. I'm coming to that big roundabout that goes on to the M1 both ways. A lorry is coming off the M1, must slow down for that…

God, I can't wait to get home to bed…

Home… to bed… to sleep…

* * * * *

The driver of the lorry could not believe his luck. He

thought he would get pulled over for sure, but no!

He chuckled. The only thing better than drinking on the job was getting away with drinking on the job.

He did not notice the car with the bent bumper until it was far too late. But by the time he had torn through it, he was too drunk to care.

It was the stupid little prick's own fault, anyway.

About the authors

Gordon Adams is a marketing consultant living near Northampton. He is the author of two non-fiction books on career change, both originally published by Infinite Ideas: *Overcoming Redundancy* (first published in 2009) and *The Great Mid-Life Career Switch* (2010). The second edition of *Overcoming Redundancy* was published in 2015 by New Generation Publishing.

Several of Gordon's short stories have been included in Northants Writers' Ink's previous anthologies. *While Glancing out of a Window* and *Talking Without Being Interrupted.*

Pat Aitcheson joined Northants Writers' Ink in 2016. She writes poetry and fiction, including short stories and longer works. She has written contemporary, horror and romance and her favourite genres are science fiction and fantasy. She is working on the sequel to her first SF novel for which she is seeking representation.

Her work appears in NWI's anthologies *While Glancing out of a Window* and *Talking without being Interrupted.* Her short story, *All the sands that touch the sea,* won 1st prize in the H E Bates Short Story Competition 2017. She posts new stories, advice and comment every week at her blog 2squarewriting.com.

As a member of the Wee Free Writers, she contributed a story for their upcoming anthology *Fire*. She contributes a story each month to the local lifestyle magazine *Barton*

Today.

Pat writes for Medium.com online, both under her own name and for several publications. She was invited to write a story for Creative Café. "Perihelion" appears in *Icons*, the first anthology from Likewise Press.

Pat lives in Northamptonshire with her family.

Deborah Bromley is a hypnotherapist specialising in Life-Between-Lives hypnotherapy, a deep trance process that connects you with memories of your life as a soul. She trained with the late Dr Michael Newton, author of the best-selling *Journey of Souls* and *Destiny of Souls*. Deborah contributed to Dr Newton's subsequent book, *Memories of the Afterlife*.

She is the author of two novels, *The Channelling Group* and *The Walk-In*. Both are available from Amazon and other online booksellers. Deborah wants to reach out to a wide audience who love paranormal fiction and share an interest in alternative realities. Her latest book is a collection of short stories, *Challenges from the Writers' Group,* and showcases pieces written in response to the various writing challenges (some fiendishly difficult) set by group members.

She has a passion for reading and is never without a stack of books on her bedside table – most likely to be crime novels, thrillers or romantic fiction. She discovered the pleasure of writing short stories after joining Northants Writers' Ink and is currently the group's secretary.

Find out more about Deborah's books by visiting

www.db-hypnosis.co.uk.

James Dart writes: I have always had a love of stories. Often in my life, I would find myself lost in a world of my own creation while sitting at home with a cup of Earl Grey or commuting home from university on the train. I eventually graduated to writing my stories down. I joined Northants Writers' Ink a few years ago and they have been extremely helpful in making me better at this art that I love so much.

The two stories under my name in this book mark the second time I have been published, the first time being in our previous anthology, *Talking Without Being Interrupted*, with the story "Nothing".

Currently, I am working on my first novel, a story set in a near-future London where the criminal reigns supreme, and a series of short stories about a pair of sorcerers who travel between parallel worlds searching for a cure to a deadly disease.

If you have enjoyed my stories, I would be extremely grateful if you keep my name in the back of your mind so that, when my current and future projects get published, you see them and think, "Oh, James Dart, I know that name." I hope you have enjoyed my stories and you will allow me to tell you more in the future.

Jason McClean enjoys writing and loves reading. He has more stories inside his head than time available to get them all down on paper.

Author influences, amongst many others, include Piers Anthony, Michael Grant, Chris Ryan, Lee Child, David Gemmell, Joe Abercrombie, Jeremy Clarkson, Stephen King, Dean Koontz, Greg Bear, Brian Cox and The Bible.

A former editor of motorcyclist specialist magazines and a Chief Reporter at *Motor Cycle News*, Jason is now happily married with two growing children and operates www.thehomeinsurer.co.uk.

With an amateur's enthusiasm for physics and a professional wonderment (or is that philosophy?) about life and the universe, Jason particularly likes writing young adult (science) fiction but enjoys challenging himself with other genres as well.

He plays the lottery once a week and has never won anything.

Michael J Richards has published *Afterwards Our Buildings Shape Us* (2014), a comic horror novel; *Bodies for Sale!* (2017), twenty weird tales; *Frank Peters: his life, times and crimes* (2017), a true crime biography; *Speaking Man to Man* (2018), twenty stories about men.

He has edited four anthologies for Northants Writers' Ink: *Tales of the Scorpion* (2015); *While Glancing out of a Window* (2016); *Talking without being Interrupted* (2017); *And Ghosts Are Real Too* (2018). He has also edited *If You Speak of Love* (2018), an anthology for Northampton Literature Group.

He chairs Northants Writers' Ink (see www.northantswritersink.net) and the Northampton

Literature Group (see www.northamptonliteraturegroup.co.uk), also leading its Writing Circle. He is Treasurer of the writers' co-operative, Northants Authors (see www.northantsauthors.com). He is a judge for the prestigious H E Bates Short Story Competition.

He studied Philosophy and Literature at Warwick University and Education at Manchester. He has lived and worked in Huntingdon, Chelmsford and Northamptonshire as a journalist, teacher, warehouseman, toilets cleaner, information manager, bookkeeper and Civil Servant.

Allan Shipham, a founder member of Northants Writers' Ink, has always used the writing challenges within the group to entertain the reader and to develop and share his unique creative skills.

For this anthology, Allan explored and researched historical events from the Dark Ages and hopes he'll also ignite your interest and curiosity.

Writing is a hobby he never thought he'd never be good enough to share. If he can, you can!

"The greatest adventure is surely a keyboard and a blank screen. What's your story?"

Rosalie J Weller writes: Short story writing is a new genre for Rosalie J Weller who prefers to write long historical fiction. Her current book project is a novel based on the life of Oliver Cromwell's wife, Elizabeth Bourchier.

Rosalie is an ordained minister of the Uniting Presbyterian Church of Southern Africa and, in this capacity, has written two Bible Study books: *David – a Man for our Times* (2018); *The Prison Letters: a Collection of Bible Studies* (2018), both available from Amazon and other good online booksellers. She is working on a third, *Tell Me the Stories of Jesus*.

Having lived in South Africa for eighteen years, she set an earlier novel, *The Greek Tycoon's Treasure* (2015), there. Written under the pseudonym Rosalie Franzel, it is also available from Amazon.

Besides writing, Rosalie is a keen book collector, particularly of Africana and can often be found browsing at book auctions and book fairs.

N M Wogden writes: I was born and raised in Barnstaple, North Devon, and moved to the Wellingborough area last year for a new job and to be closer to my partner.

I have been writing science fiction fantasy for several years now but I am still trying to get my first book published.

I joined Northants Writers' Ink last year in order to improve my writing style and to get some peer reviews about my work and ways to improve it.

Chris Wright is an IT analyst and programmer, based in Wellingborough. He is married to Karen and has three grown children and four growing grandchildren.

With an educational background in maths and computing, he has always had a keen interest in both reading and viewing science fiction. Writing was a later development, science fiction the natural destination.

Northants Writers' Ink has been a great help both in developing his skills and broadening the genres that he's willing to tackle. The short story presented here is his second foray into the published world, several shorter works appearing in the group's 2017 anthology.

He is treasurer of Northants Writers' Ink.

Tales of the Scorpion

an anthology by Northants Writers' Ink

Tales of the Scorpion is a collection of short stories and poems, each with a twist or sting in the tail.

Stories include *Guido's Door*, a disturbing story about a haunted prison; *Queen of Swords*, a tale about emotionally confused Tarot readers; *Deborah's Diary*, the secrets of a mass murderer; *A Different Type of Service*, one of several stories featuring passionate love triangles; *Making an English Lady*, fun and frolics at a mediaeval orgy; *Learnin' the Family Business*, the blooding of a young member of the Mafia set in 1920s' New York.

Thirteen stories and ten poems comprise this first anthology from Northants Writers' Ink, a writers' group from Wellingborough, Northamptonshire, England.

What they said about

Tales of the Scorpion

"Readers with a nervous disposition or those who see life through rose tinted spectacles beware. This book is unsettling… I found it compelling and was anxious to know the conclusion each time… "

"A wonderful book to pick up when you have a few minutes to spare in the hectic world."

"… if you like horror and the creepy and unpleasant, you'll like this."

"… anyone interested in well-told stories (with perhaps a touch of darkness in places) should investigate."

Available from Amazon and all good online booksellers.

While Glancing out of a Window

an anthology by Northants Writers' Ink

45 short stories. 9 poems. 2 scripts. 1 essay. 9 authors. Crime and drama. Ghost and horror. History and myth. Humour and whimsy. Science fiction. Love and romance.

While Glancing out of a Window is Northants Writers' Ink's 2nd anthology.

What they said about

While Glancing out of a Window

"… it overflows with creativity and a passion for writing, clever story lines and some excellent descriptive text."

"Do buy this book. Really worth reading."

"I'm impressed by the variety of voices and subject matter and would recommend this as a great read."

Available from Amazon and all good online booksellers.

Talking without being Interrupted

an anthology by Northants Writers' Ink

- Murder on TV's reality show *Celebrity House*.
- A painter sells his soul in exchange for artistic perfection.
- A dying man yearns for his lost love.
- A girl wanders isolated streets, chased by an unnamed monster.
- An epicure's hunt for unusual food takes her where she least expects it.
- Game shows replace General Elections to decide who runs the country.
- A boy becomes a superhero and finds it's not all it's cracked up to be.
- A daughter looking after her aging parent finds their roles are reversed.
- Is Rose's new boyfriend a serial killer? Surely not! Can't be.
- Violet, the Kray Twins' mother, meets Judy Garland.
- An office worker's mystical experience in an art gallery.
- Love, loss and sacrifice in a north Arctic community.

What they said about

Talking without being Interrupted

"This is the third anthology from this writers group, and once again there is something for every reader. Great to dip into over a coffee break or before bed, the 52 pieces range from whimsical to gritty, covering the range of human experience. Romance, crime, drama, horror, science fiction, humour, poetry are all strongly represented. If you don't want to commit to reading a novel length work, there's sure to be something here to entertain you."

"The quality of this anthology is just as good, if not better, than the previous one. It gives the same great variety of stories. I still haven't read them all, but there's plenty more to look forward to which I can dip into anytime. Everyone can find a favourite in this mix, and even step out of their reading comfort zone and pick stories at random."

"I loved this third anthology from this group of local writers. Such variety and so entertaining. Something for everyone. I also enjoyed the second anthology - While Glancing out of a Window. Each story makes you think. They are so inventive! I am a fan of the flash fiction and (spoiler alert) I had to quote a line from Nick Johns' By the Light of the Silvery Moon: 'I'd only bitten her, see, not eaten her.' You have to read on to find out more and you won't be disappointed."

Printed in Great Britain
by Amazon

19551825R00103